HIGH PLAINS AMBUSH

Eli Holten, at the head of twenty screaming, painted warriors thundered over the saddle notch and down on the astonished outlaws. Swiftly the range closed, so that the hardcase gang became trapped between two hostile forces. The volume of fire increased from the soldiers on the one side, lashing into the huddled desperados. Of the twenty-five remaining, three died quick and hard.

"Swing wide," Holten yelled. "Cut off any escape!"

With the range closing, Eli Holten scabbarded his Winchester and drew the conversion model Remington Army revolver. It was like a shooting gallery for the attacking forces. Targets abounded.

And blood soaked the parched plains.

THE SCOUT

#31

BUCK GENTRY
HARD RIDER

ZEBRA BOOKS
KENSINGTON PUBLISHING CORP.

ZEBRA BOOKS

are published by

Kensington Publishing Corp.
475 Park Avenue South
New York, NY 10016

First printing: August, 1990

Printed in the United States of America

Special acknowledgements to Mark K. Roberts

"I have always had a particular admiration for my scouts, who played a critical role in sniffing out the enemy and in acting as messengers. In particular, William F. Cody who, during the frigid winter campaign of '68 made a heroic series of horseback rides of some 350 miles in about 60 hours, through terrain infested with Indians, where several couriers had previously been killed."

—Lt. Gen. Philip H. Sheridan
Memoirs

CHAPTER 1

Thick and virginally white, a pristine mantle lay heavily across the Dakota plains. Here and there the wind had made itself visible in the swirls of its copperplate signature along the open faces of the drifts. The last—at least everyone hoped it would be the last—snow of the winter had fallen over an eighteen hour period, blanketing the prairie in glistening alabaster. Small dots moved from place to place, spread widely over a roughly defined square, one mile on a side. Slowly they resolved into nearly identical bay horses and blue-uniformed riders.

With care, evidencing some apparent need for hurry, they ranged over the landscape like splendid pointers coursing the field for game birds. Their bent heads soon indicated they searched for something that must lie beneath the ten inches of snow they traversed.

"If he's in a drift, we won't find him for at least a week," a veteran frontier sergeant confided to two men flapping gloved hands together to restore warmth and circulation.

"Nobody could live that long, Sarge," a moon-faced private with round, gold-rimmed spectacles observed unnecessarily.

"Hmmm. That's brilliant, Carter," The NCO replied sarcastically. "A right fucking genius. Why the hell you

7

think we're wastin' the time of two entire companies searching?"

"Wouldn't think a gen'ral would be out in this kind of shit," the four-eyed trooper opined.

"It wasn't snowing when he left Fort Rawlins," the noncom observed. "And it still wasn't when that prospector came upon him. Only it looks like the ol' coot didn't mark the spot good as he claimed."

An exuberant shout interrupted the conversation, and a moment later an excited trooper floundered through the belly-high drifts to where Sergeant McMasters waited. He held one arm aloft, clutching a length of slender pole and a snow-encrusted, rigidly frozen scrap of red cloth.

"We found this, First Sergeant. It's the marker," he added needlessly.

McMasters studied it. "Hmmm. Just like the old boy said. You see anything else? Find anything? A lump in the snow or something?"

"No, First Sergeant. Nothin' at all around the marker. If that red stuff hadn't been froze, stickin' straight up like, we'd not found this."

"It's a start." To the idlers beside him, McMasters issued curt orders. "Take word to the rest of the men. Have them close in on the point where this marker was found and search there."

"Yes, First Sergeant," both privates responded.

McMasters pulled a hard, thick, uninvitingly black cigar from the pocket of his tunic and clamped it between large, yellowed teeth. A scrape along his belt buckle fired a lucifer, with which he ignited the tube of hand-rolled tobacco. Blue-tinged smoke wreathed his head a moment later. The troops redeployed and continued the search, this time with considerably more energy.

The old man was well liked, McMasters reflected. If he wasn't, the troops wouldn't be making this much effort in this sort of weather. He drew deeply on his

8

cigar, exhaled and watched the smoke blend with the vapor of his breath. Suddenly one of the figures fired three shots into the air, and the others spurred their mounts. Quickly the soldiers converged, horses surging in sparkling sprays of snow flakes through the belly-deep drifts. First Sergeant McMasters, 12th U.S. Cavalry, rolled the stogie from one side of his mouth to the other, then urged his mount forward. He didn't have to cover more than half the distance to know that the object of their search had been found.

General Frank Corrington, commanding Fort Rawlins, Dakota Territory, lay huddled in a welter of red-stained snow. His body drawn up in a fetal ball, he showed no signs of life except for the continued slow seep of blood from his wounds. Sergeant McMasters swung from the saddle and knelt beside the man he had faithfully followed for more than fifteen years. Gently he lifted the grizzled head and cradled it on his knee.

"Gen'ral, Gen'ral, can you hear me, sir?" McMasters asked urgently. Then, bending close, he spoke in almost a whisper. "Jesus, Frank, why'd they do this? Who was it?"

General Frank Corrington lay there, his life still oozing out of his wounds. When he made no sign of hearing or understanding, McMasters looked up with a haunted expression.

"Bring two horses. Rig a litter. Somebody get that field medical kit. We've gotta patch him up some before we move out."

Major Wallace Jansen stood over the operating platform, which more closely resembled an autopsy table than a surgical bed, and stared down at the bruised, frostbitten, bullet-holed body of his long-time friend and commaning officer. A horse-drawn litter had brought General Frank Corrington back to Fort Rawlins less than an hour ago. Jansen had set to work at once. For all his efforts, he had little to show.

He had stopped the bleeding. Large, fat bandages covered the bullet wounds. Snow-packed gauze dressings had been wrapped around toes, fingertips and ears to slowly thaw frostbitten flesh. Maj. Wallace Jansen felt utterly defeated. For the first time in his career he allowed personal feelings to invade his professional demeanor. His eyes burned and stung, from tightly repressed tears as well as from long, intense effort under inadequate lighting. Only slowly did he become aware of the other post officers crowding the room.

"Gentlemen, General Corrington is alive and resting quietly now. How long he will continue to live is in the hands of God. I've done everything I can . . . for now. There's a bullet needs removing, but not now. He hasn't the strength to survive the operation."

"What happened?" Colonel Britton, the brigade executive officer, demanded. "Did he come around long enough to say?"

"No, Colonel. I'm sorry to say he's in a coma and only barely reacts to what tests we have to determine responses. Although I'm not a forensic practitioner, I'va had enough experience with wounds as an army surgeon to make an educated guess." Major Jansen paused a moment and ran slim, soft surgeon's fingers through his mop of shaggy red-brown hair.

"The general has been shot, three times. One in the left shoulder, probably the first wound he received, which may or may not have knocked him from his horse. The second in his abdomen, I would judge to have been inflicted to, ah, torture him, so's to speak. In between them, he was savagely beaten, probably interrogated by . . . someone. There is another bullet gouge along the side of his skull. It parted the flesh clear to the bone. No doubt it was meant to kill him and is the cause of his deep coma. He has been treated, except for the bullet in his shoulder, and is resting as

10

well—as well as possible, considering. As of now, that's all I can tell you."

"Thank you, Doctor," Colonel Britton spoke for the staff and regimental officers present. "Please keep us informed."

"Of course."

A man of middling stature, at five-nine, kept step with Colonel Britton as they crossed the parade ground. His blond, wispy, almost snow-white hair fluttered in the breeze under his field kapi. At thirty-eight, he was considered quite young to command a regiment of cavalry. Lt. Colonel Howard Mayberry kept his gaze distant, the heat in his steely gray eyes enough to melt the armor off the *Monitor*.

"Goddammit!" he swore. "Why did this have to happen to Frank?"

"I'd say the same, but that would be repetitious," Colonel Britton agreed. "Generals make enemies. Frank had more than his fair share. It could be any one of them for any number of reasons. More to the point, what now?"

"We need someone who knew Frank, and knew his enemies well enough to provide some sort of clue. I'm contacting Eli Holten."

"Hell, Holten is in Arizona Territory," Colonel Britton reminded him.

"And his best friend is in there hanging on to life by a strand of hair. If anyone can help us, help Frank, now, it's Eli Holten."

"Holten's under orders; he can't simply take off to come up here."

"I've got that one covered, too, Sam. I'll send another telegram to Department Headquarters, explaining the situation and asking that orders be cut releasing Holten from the Department of Arizona."

Sam Britton grinned for the first time since General Corrington had come up missing. "Georgie Crook isn't

11

going to like this. But I'll sign that one myself."

"Too bad for Crook. Right now we have no other choice."

Sunlight, intensified as it reflected off the two-foot layer of snow, streamed through the window. At its altitude, Globe, Arizona Territory, remained in the grip of winter. The sun, though rich and warm, occupied a sky of pale, winter blue. Piñon logs crackled on the open hearth and in a small, potbelly cast-iron stove in the spacious bedroom. Two distinctly feminine hands, though not a pair, grasped Eli Holten's engorged phallus. Slowly, in perfect rhythm, they stroked him up and down.

Holten sighed. Such was life, and the sacrifices one must make, for a contract civilian scout assigned to Department Headquarters, Department of Arizona. He certainly had it rough. Oh, he'd be first to admit that.

"Ummmm. A little faster, please?" he requested of the delightful duo who administered to his turgid organ. "That's right, girls."

Ah, yes, it was *girls,* decidedly in the plural. Concha Ocampo, naked as the day she was born, sprawled across his bare, hard, flat belly, gripping the lower third of his ample endowment. Suspended over his muscular legs on one elbow, a naughtily nude Cherry Blaze encased the next third in the delicate fingers of her left hand. The remaining, unattended, tertiary part thrust upward in the warm, pine resin scented air.

Not for long, though, as Concha squiggled herself into a better position and lowered her shapely head, long, raven tresses spilling forward over her shoulders to brush Eli's thighs. A lightning bolt of raw pleasure jolted Eli's body as her soft, moist lips closed over the exposed, ruby tip of his manhood. Feather-light, her tongue slid across sensitive flesh.

12

"Aaah! Aaah, Connie," Holten gasped. "You always know how to amaze me."

Another tongue got into the game, licking the reddened skin of his shaft, between hand and lips. Eli Holten shivered with delight. His heart rate increased noticeably, and his mouth went dry.

"Girls, *GIRLS!*" he pleaded in a croak. "I thought we ruled out torture. Didn't we?"

A kittenish purr came from fully occupied Concha. Cherry produced a low, sexy chuckle deep in her throat. "This isn't torture, beloved. We only want to make you happy."

"If I got any happier, I'd die, and my soul would fly away to Valhalla."

Cherry made a pouting kiss. "Only warriors go to Valhalla. You're just a scout for the army."

"I do my share of fighting," Holten responded in mock offense.

"We know," Cherry said only a bit sharply. "Your body has plenty of—of evidence."

His scars had always troubled Cherry Blaze. The young, carefree madam of a luxurious bordello known as the Knob Hill Social Club let little in life affect her, but the various puckered circles, jagged lines and small depressions in Eli Holten's hide had upset her enough to make obvious exception. Despite their unsettling presence, she clearly loved him. Loved him enough to share his passion with another woman—and gloriously at the same time.

Although no stranger to a *ménage à trois,* Holten could not remember enjoying so deliriously happy a multiple partner encounter outside of the remarkable talents of the five energetic and inventive Thorne sisters. He shuddered in response to the unceasing stimulus of the hungry mouths of Cherry and Concha. Undinted after two hours of the bedroom antics—their marvelous affair began shortly after a light noon meal—passion radiated from all three. Cherry broke

13

off with a loud smack.

"Now. I've got to have him now," she pleaded.

Concha obligingly rearranged herself, to lie full length atop an over-charged Eli. Her creamy thighs extended beyond his head, toes snubbed up against the wall. Cherry straddled him and lowered her moist, fevered cleft until she made the first, ecstatic contact with his hot lance. With excrutiating slowness she impaled herself, while Concha licked frantically at the exposed portion of his mighty shaft. Holten breathed deeply, gathering strength.

Sweet and tart, with a whiff of salt, Concha's feminine aroma surrounded Eli's head and made him giddy. Her nearly hairless mound hung only inches from his face. His tongue flicked out and parted the pouting lips. While Concha wriggled and renewed her efforts on his bulging maleness, Holten probed farther.

Suddenly restraint exploded for all three, and they went into a state of sublime agitation, tendering to each other all the skillful artifices of their combined experience. With a whirl, the real world streaked away. Bounding among the constellations, driven into a state of euphoria by individual and cumulative novalike stimulation, mutual completion burst upon the exultant lovers with rosy exuberance.

Churning emotions gave birth to mews and squeals of rapture, groans and wails of celestial bliss. Slowly, shakily, the quaking lovers recaptured the trappings of ever-present reality. For a long while, no one spoke. Then Holten rose on one elbow.

"Oh, my, there's parts of me that keep saying I'm getting too old for this sort of thing."

"But not this part," Concha responded teasingly as she tweeked his still-rigid member.

"Or this," Cherry murmured. Her lips spread, then flattened as she lovingly kissed his distended scrotum.

From a cloud of pink-fleshed jubilance, Holten spoke philosophically. "How—how is it that the two of you, who have never known each other before, could bring yourselves to sh-share so completely?"

"I don' know," Concha responded, still having some trouble with English pronunciation. "It jus' seem like a good idea."

"I suppose . . . I think it's because we haven't known each other for a long while. No habit of competing," Cherry offered. "And you're enough for any two—no, three women."

Five, Holten thought, irrelevantly remembering the auburn-haired Thorne girls again. The last time they had been together, the five sisters working on him separately and together had quickly drained him of all his energies. The memory brought a smile.

"Don't get smug on us, mister," Cherry cautioned.

"I was . . . remembering," Eli defended.

"I am happy to give you sometheeng to remember," Concha allowed, hugging him.

"Concha, dear, I think it's time we had some girl-talk," Cherry suggested with a definite glint in her eyes.

"You wan' make up a new way to keep Eli happy?" Concha asked eagerly.

Cherry nodded. "You've got the right idea. Every time we're together, we should have some way to . . . well—don't listen to this, Eli," she pleaded.

"I'll cover my ears," Holten offered, raising his big, wide hands to his head.

Cherry reached out and ruffled his long, curly blond hair. "That won't do a damn bit of good. Why don't you go out and get us all a drink from the kitchen? I could use a nibble, too. Good loving makes me hungry."

Holten removed himself from the bed and slid into trousers. He left the bedroom of Concha's pleasant adobe house and turned toward the rear, where the outside door gave access to the detached kitchen. A knock at the front interrupted his progress. On bare feet he padded to the stout oak portal.

15

"What is it?" he growled as he swung back the door.

Blinking in surprise, a shaggy-haired youngster of eleven or twelve stood there, a familiar yellow envelope in his left hand. His eyes widened at the sight of Eli's bare, scar-checked chest. "You *are* Eli Holten," he blurted in an awed tone.

"Was the last time I checked. That for me?"

"Yessir. From the army."

Holten examined the freckled face. "C'mon in, boy. I may have an answer to send."

"Yessir." Moving in the partial paralysis of his hero worship, the lad stepped inside, oblivious to the fact his hero was wearing only his trousers.

From beyond the man he considered a legend, giggles reached his ears. The boy cocked his head in curiosity and identified two separate pitches. Two? He rejected that idea out of hand.

"What is it, *amado?*" Concha called.

"Yes, Eli, who's at the door?"

Son of a bitch! It is two, the kid thought in astonishment.

"Telegram from McDowell," Eli informed the ladies. "Seems I'm temporarily detatched from duty. Wait, there's another one." Holten unfolded the second missive, the one from Fort Rawlins, and scanned it in haste. Then he read it slower, his expression growing grimmer with each word. His face thunderous, he at last remembered the boy and turned to him.

"Have Ruben send a plain acknowledgement to Fort McDowell. In reply to the other, say I'm leaving immediately. Will take fastest route there." He handed the boy a two and a half dollar gold piece. "That should do it, and keep the change."

"Yes, sir, m-mighty generous of you, Mr. Holten."

Taking his astonishment with him, the boy left with Holten's largess. More puzzling than the size of the tip he would be bound to get was consideration of what he had discovered inside. How could anyone, even so famous a scout as Eli Holten, be so lucky as to service two women at the same time? How? The best he could manage so far, he thought with a twinge of jealousy, was to play stink-finger with li'l Suzie Brown while she flogged his log out behind the barn. But then, every kid had played stink-finger with Suzie Brown. Gosh, two at once. How would he work that?

In the comfortable house on the edge of Globe, the lascivious ladies presented another and immediate problem to Eli. Neither could see the importance of ending their tryst so abruptly. Both sulked and pouted while Holten carefully dressed, part of his mind absent, planning what he would take and how he would go. Frank Corrington on the edge of death; Eli needed in Dakota? What could have happened?

"Eli," Cherry complained loudly, "it just isn't fair."

"Life isn't fair, my sweet Cherry," Holten offered lightly.

"What difference does it make if this general is injured?" she persisted.

"It makes a whole hell of a lot," Eli snapped, his temper reviving and wearing thin in the afterglow of their loving. "Frank is my oldest and best friend, also my commander for more years than I care to remember. I owe that man."

"The army is letting you go?" Concha asked. "They would not do that for anyone else."

"Which only points out the importance," Holten argued.

"But, Eli," his lovely delights wailed simultaneously.

"Enough, dammit. I've got too much on my mind right now. I'm going, I'm doing so right now and there's nothing that will prevent me."

His harsh tone and fixed expression brooked no attempt at compromise. Cherry and Concha waited in silence while Eli made ready to leave the house. He warmly kissed them both, without their returning the tenderness.

"I'll be back. Don't worry about that," he vowed at the door.

They waited until he had ridden a block away before they dissolved into tears. Wailing over their mutual loss, they hugged each other closely and rocked on the bed that still gave off the aroma of their recent passion. Eli Holten was gone.

CHAPTER 2

Two companies of cavalry swung into their saddles like a single man. Crisp commands put them into a column of twos, and they walked their mounts out the main gate of Fort Rawlins for a couple of hours of mounted drill. Their places were taken on the parade ground by a company of recruits from the 11th Infantry Regiment. Fresh from the infantry center at Fort Snelling, Minnesota, the ninety-seven new men had only the most basic of military skills. Bellows-lunged sergeants began bawling orders. Corporals with limber, willow swagger sticks aided the learning process with sharp, stinging smacks to the backs of legs and posteriors. Inside the headquarters building, two men stood before a large map of the territory, faces grim.

"All hell's breaking loose in the Black Hills," Colonel Britton snapped. "And we stand here with our thumbs up our asses."

He pointed to the small, red flags stuck into the map by pins. Lieutenant Colonel Mayberry nodded solemnly. With one thick, weather-reddened finger he tapped on an area outlined in green.

"Here's what we have to worry about the most. Pine Ridge Agency has been a focus for hostile activity since the day it was established. If that changes, we can be sure of big trouble."

"You underestimate the Indian Police and our garrisons at the agencies, Howie. They handled the Crazy Horse problem without an uprising. Surely they can contain any mass movement toward jumping the reservations."

Lieutenant Colonel Mayberry's lips curled in wry contempt. "Yeah, Sam, and in a manner that cost us the services of Eli Holten. Besides, those garrisons are under direct control from Headquarters. The geniuses with all the stars in St. Paul send poor sods like those out to the agencies to gain experience." He nodded toward the window and, by implication, the recruits on the parade. "You have to keep that in mind, as well as this. Although they have been shoved onto reservations, the Sioux and Cheyenne still consider the Black Hills, the *Hesapa* as the Sioux call them, sacred. Their access to the *Hesapa* has been severely restricted by the treaty, but they still have access." Mayberry paused and paced from the map to Colonel Britton's desk.

Lifting a paper, he went on. "We can accept these reports as accurate. They came from Corporal Newcomb and his Crow scouts. All the white riffraff of the frontier seem to be pouring into the Hills. Wherever they go, Indians, any Indians, are being shot at on sight throughout the Hills, even if in the treaty-grant areas. How long before the Sioux get pissed off? Angry young men who already consider themselves cheated out of their ancestoral rights to the Sun Dance by the treaty are slipping off the reservations to attack white prospectors in retaliation. If this keeps on, we'll for sure step into a big, wet cow pattie."

"There, up there! That's where it has to be coming from," one gold-crazed prospector yelled, pointing uphill.

After two hours of panning the stream that

20

meandered around the base of a low, round mount, he and his three friends had retrieved nearly a half pound of gold from the gravelly bottom. It promised a great deal more farther up the stream, particularly above them on the flat-topped hill. Everything about the formation indicated the possibility of a rich vein, perhaps two or three not far below ground. Eager to learn, the four prospectors clambered up the steep grade.

At the top they stopped in consternation and superstitious awe. Fully two dozen platforms rose on tall, notched lodgepole pine supports. Each held the wrapped corpse of a Sioux. Some showed the ravages of time, being mere scraps of bone and sun-dried flesh, tatters of buckskin clothing. Others could have been put there less than a month ago. Feathered shields, bows and quivers of arrows awaited the fallen to take up in the Spirit World. One of the prospectors whipped the hat from his head and crossed himself.

"Jesus, Mary and Joseph," he spoke in a whisper. "'Tis an Injun burial ground."

"So what," a less religious companion barked. "Let's clear some of this shit away an' start digging test holes."

"No, that's not a good idea, lad," the faithful Irishman protested. "This be sacred ground to the Injuns."

"Yeah, but not to us. You're a mackerel-snapper, and me an' the boys ain't nothing, so don't matter a hill of beans. C'mon, bring up the tools and we can get goin'."

Two hours went by in energetic labor. Almost exactly like the glowing flyers back East had described it, in the words of the late George Armstrong Custer, nuggets literally clung to the roots of grass. Driven by their greed and the lust for gold, the prospectors quickly forgot the sanctity of their location. They didn't even bother to set a careful watch.

Which nearly proved their undoing when seven

young Sioux warriors, seeking inspiration and approval from the Spirits, came to the mount to pray. They rode up the easy, western slope and topped the rise in silence. Their first sight of the burial place of their ancestors included four white men engaged in desecrating the site.

Swiftly, rage filled the nominal leader. *"Wicaśaśnia,"* he spat.

"All white men are without honor, Elk Runner," another asserted.

Quickly Elk Runner formulated a plan. So far the whites had not seen them. He motioned for his companions to come with him. *"Hakamya upo,"* he commanded.

They followed closely as directed. Once in position, Elk Runner raised his trade rifle above his head and quickly brought it down in the signal to attack. From three directions the Sioux warriors charged the burial ground.

"Huka hey! Huka hey!" Elk Runner shrieked at the top of his lungs. *"Hu ihpeya wacayapo!"*

Stricken, the prospectors looked up to see the warriors thundering toward them. In an instant they had dropped their shovels and picks and snatched up rifles. With deadly accuracy they began to fire. One young brave, a boy really, screamed and spun sideways off his pony. Another grunted and glanced down at a wound in his shoulder.

"Kay-iiiiiya-iiiiii!" came another war cry.

With methodical speed, the prospectors levered rounds into the chambers of their rifles and squeezed triggers. Unsteady fire answered them. Elk Runner surged to the front and swung his five remaining companions in through the area where the prospectors worked. He struck one with his rifle barrel; another he smacked on the side of the head with a steel tomahawk. At the far side of the flat top, the Sioux wheeled their mounts and streaked back.

They met a blizzard of hot lead. Bullets snapped past; others plucked at flesh, downed a charging pony, and killed three more warriors. Short on ammunition, Elk Runner lowered his rifle, so that it hung by a rawhide thong from his war saddle, and readied his bow. His surviving friends did the same. Arrows clattered among the besieged white men. Quickly the distance narrowed between warring factions. Elk Runner loosed another arrow.

It struck the Irish prospector in the chest. He fell on one side, hands clutching the shaft where it entered his body. "Oh, my God, I am heartily sorry for having offended Thee," he muttered weakly.

His companions triggered another volley. Now only two of the Sioux remained alive. Elk Runner and another brave quickly noted the situation and drummed heels into their ponies' sides.

"They're runnin'!" one of the gold-seekers shouted.

"Aye," the Irish one spoke softly. "An' sure it is, I'm dyin'. 'Tis punishment for desecratin' this place. Ah, lads—lads, it's sorry I. . . ."

"Jesus, Patrick's dead."

Unaffected by the loss, a hard-faced prospector glanced at the dead man and after the fleeing Sioux. "They won't bother us again. Let's get to digging."

Colonel Britton paced the floor of his office. "It's official now. This just came in from headquarters." He gestured to Lieutenant Colonel Mayberry with a telegraph message form. "Effective upon receipt," he read aloud. "Elements of the Nineth Brigade are not, repeat not, to initiate actions against alleged treaty violators in the Black Hills region of Dakota Territory. All efforts are to be made to keep potentially hostile natives under constant observation. In the event of hostile action, such hostiles as are encountered are to be suppressed in the most vigorous manner. The territorial government will conduct any necessary investigations into alleged treaty violation."

"Goddamn them," Mayberry blurted. "One would think that after all that's gone on, even those stuffed-pants desk soldiers would realize we have an explosive situation to deal with. Especially after that last incident in the burial ground. Five Sioux young men killed. Do they actually think the Oglala and Sans Arc will stand around mumbling about it? And what's that about the territorial government? That collection of failed lawyers and snake oil peddlers is more than likely responsible for bringing all these new people here."

"We'll find out soon enough, Howie. There's one of them out in the orderly room. Will you ask the sergeant major to show him in. A Mr., ah, Ashford."

A few moments later, a punctilious, prim and proper young man entered the office. He might have been in his mid-thirties, Howard Mayberry judged. He certainly was every inch the modern, efficient bureaucrat. His watery blue eyes twinkled behind thick lenses held in place by gold wire rims.

"I am Mason Ashford, General," he declared with a slight lisp, extending one hand at the end of a limp wrist.

"General Corrington is indisposed. I am the executive officer, Colonel Britton."

"Oh, that is a shame," Ashford burbled, leaving both officers wondering if he referred to the general's condition or to having to talk to the second in command.

"Mr. Ashford," Colonel Britton began calmly, "I have received a message from our headquarters at St. Paul that I find confusing, not to mention astonishing. In it I am informed that any investigation of, or punative action against, violators of the Black Hills Treaty with the Sioux are to be conducted by civilian authority, in this case, your territorial government."

"That is correct. As confidential secretary to the

territorial governor, I have been privy to the delicate negotiations that accomplished this most necessary step toward rectifying the errors of the past."

Colonel Britton cocked his head to one side. "I'm sorry, that doesn't quite make sense. What errors?"

Ashford spread his hands in a feminine gesture, his lips disappearing as he attempted to put steel into his words. "Why, the interference by the army into strictly civilian areas of responsibility. The duplication of effort. The enormous expense of maintaining a large field force of troops in what is fully acknowledged as a time of peace."

Britton scowled; Mayberry stifled a guffaw. Colonel Britton struggled to keep his voice calm, unemotional. "Our primary function is to police this territory. Besides, I've been here long enough to recall when the citizens, including the territorial government, came to the army on bended knee. They whined and sniveled for us to 'Please, please protect us from the savages.' Well, we protected them. We still are. And, by God, if we don't do something to drive those interlopers off the Black Hills, we'll have us an uprising on our hands that will make the Custer battle look like a Wednesday night prayer meeting."

Ashford pursed his lips. "It's this sort of bellicose, antiquated thinking that must be eradicated. Fortunately you are no longer in charge of the conduct of such affairs."

Lieutenant Colonel Mayberry added support to his acting commander. "Dammit, man, that wave of invading prospectors and the like represents a clear and immediate danger to the peace and stability you're prattling about."

A petulent sniff answered him. "I fail to find any threat, real or implied, in these bold, adventurous Americans who are bringing the blessings of white civilization to the Black Hills. Need I say that I speak for the governor as well? Be assured, if we find any real violators of the treaty, they shall be swiftly punished. However, men in peaceful pursuit of their chosen livelihood can hardly be considered treaty violators."

Colonel Britton couldn't believe what he heard. "Do you call the murder of five Sioux young men in a burial ground 'peaceful'?"

Ashford lifted one long, slim hand to daintily suppress a yawn. "From what I hear, they fired first. Besides, they were only Indians. I think this interview is over, gentlemen." Ashford started for the door, paused and turned back. "At least you have received your orders. I trust that the governor can, in future, rely upon you to obey them."

"Son of a bitch!" Lieutenant Colonel Mayberry exclaimed after the prissy bureaucrat had departed.

"Yeah, Howie. Him? Or the ones he represents?" Colonel Britton asked archly.

Far to the west of Fort Rawlins, on the tumble-down homestead of Gabriel Thorne, five lovely young ladies, aged fourteen to nineteen, gathered for a family conference before the large, stone fireplace. Outside, water dripped from the eaves, and rotting clumps of snow hid in the shadowed places. The rough lane that led to the house from the main road had become a quagmire. There in the common room—living room/kitchen/dining room—a cheery fire of pine logs snapped and crackled. Her copper hair done in large sausage curls, the eldest, Melissa, directed the conversation.

"Y'all feel just like I do. I can tell. We've all got the itch somethin' terrible."

Doreen, at eighteen, produced a knowing smile. "Ain't been anybody along in some while that could ease it for us."

Samantha and Susanna turned identical sixteen-year-old faces to their eldest sister. "Them Cheyenne boys don't count," they said in chorus. Then Susanna, the dominant twin, explained further. "Too young and not enough experience. Both of 'em squealed like pigs. Bet they never had it before."

"They didn't," Helen, the youngest, piped up. "One of them told me. Peter's all right in an emergency, but with Paw ailin' he's gone with Matt, Mark an' Luke for the spring calving. Paul's not much better'n those Cheyenne boys—too little an' not enough 'sperience. What we need—" she brightened—"what we need is—"

"We know what we need," Samantha said through a giggle. "What we need is to do something about it. Only . . . what?"

"Paul's gone off to run his traps, so there's no one in the family to make decisions but us," Melissa told them. "Supplies are runnin' low, and there's no cash money at hand. We gotta get help for a whole lot more than our itches."

"Where can we get it?" Doreen asked plaintively.

Unaware that the subject she was about to introduce had been gone for nearly two years, Helen let the words pop out. "I know. I tried to tell you before. We can get help at Fort Rawlins. What we need is Eli Holten."

A lowbed rattled along the main street of Pierre, Dakota Territory. On it rested two damaged buck-boards on their way to the wainwright's for repair. Maw Setterly had been careless with her henhouse again, and chickens picked at the bits of undigested grain in the fresh, smoking, green horse dung. A gaggle of children of indeterminate sex rushed like a dust-devil around the corner where the Farmers and Drovers Bank dominated the intersection with First Avenue.

In an office on the third floor of the bank, the only three-story, brick building in town, Mason Ashford sat primly on the edge of a Regency chair. Three men occupied the room with him, one seated behind a large slab desk, with the others to either side in thronelike wing chairs. Heavy burgundy drapes and louvered blinds muted the sounds of commercial bluster below. Amos Wade patted the desk surface almost affectionately and spoke in a clear, tenor voice that still managed to crackle with power.

"You can assure the governor that the continued desecration of sacred sites will soon have the Sioux on the warpath. The Cheyenne are already raising hell west of here."

"And how soon do you predict we can file claims on that gold-rich land? Governor Stratton is extremely anxious about establishing Strattonberg. Ah, that will be the, ah, boomtown in the western Black Hills to which the governor has modestly lent his name," Ashford stated.

Zacharia Walters, a small man with a head of thick, curly, salt-and-pepper hair, chuckled and drew on a long, fat cigar. His thin lips grew even thinner when he spoke. "I admire men of such overweening modesty."

Ashford *tisked* censoriously. "Governor Stratton no doubt has his reasons."

"Oh, I'm sure he does," Zach Walters allowed. His close-set, icy eyes glittered with malice above the sharp slash of his nose. "The main point is that none of us profits from this enterprise until we achieve every goal outlined at the beginning."

"That includes getting rid of that officious bastard, Frank Corrington," Hezakiah Manning, youngest of the unholy trio, asserted. "He actually believes that treaties with Indians are meant to be honored."

Amos Wade turned cold, hard, flat brown eyes on Zach Walters. "I still say it's a mistake to kill a brigadier general in the U.S. Army. At least *this* one, unless we manage to get Eli Holten, too."

"Who is this Holten person?" Ashford asked in his prim voice.

"A bad piece of business for anyone who crosses him," Wade explained, one hand massaging the bald pate that shone above a gray-black fringe that resembled a monk's tonsure. "And killing Frank Corrington will definitely cross him."

"Well, I have rather disturbing news for you. Some of your hirelings have already made an attempt on Corrington's life. Whoever you sent to dispose of that meddling do-gooder made a terrible mess of it. General Corrington is still alive, although in a coma. The army surgeon says he may come out of it at any time."

Visions of the cold, damp prison cell from which he had so recently been released flashed through Amos Wade's mind. The expression they produced gave him the look of a man who had bitten into something extremely foul.

"Then we should make another try. This time it had better succeed."

CHAPTER 3

Lulled by the rhythmic click-clack of the coach trucks on the Kansas and Pacific Daylight Express, Eli Holten leaned back in his plush, maroon velvet bench chair. His head nodded in time with the jolt and sway of the railroad car until his chin grounded on his chest. Sonny, his big, black Morgan stallion, was comfortably quartered—*uncomfortably* from a horse's point of view—in the stock car forward, behind the express coach. The Daylight had left Denver shortly after eleven that morning, setting a new record of only being fifteen minutes late.

After a satisfactory mid-day meal, Eli had returned to the sleeper car, made up now into its daytime role with double-sided, plush bench seats. Warm sunlight pouring through the window at an acute angle helped induce the scout's drowsiness. Poised on the beginning of an ear-rattling snore, Eli was saved from embarrassment by a twittering female voice.

"Oh, there you are, Mr. Holten." Mrs. Leland York might have posed for a *Harper's* engraving of the "proper matron."

Wagnerian stout, the buxom dowager added to the impression of barrellike vastness by affecting a tight, black dress with yards of lace flounces and a gigantic feather boa of midnight hue. Jet ostrich feathers adorned her heavily vailed, picture hat. More disturb-

30

ing to Eli Holten's way of seeing things was the ample trace of mustache on the firm upper lip of the hard-faced woman.

"Snaar-ZAK!" Holten jolted awake. "Oh, Mrs. York. Yes, yes, I must have drifted off. Wonderful place for a nap, these trains."

If Eli Holten sounded unlike himself, it could be forgiven him. Not one to speak frivolously, he blamed the zany response on the current object of his attention. Certainly not Mrs. Leland York. Definitely her sixteen-year-old daughter, Victoria. Judging from his offspring, Leland York must be a painfully handsome man. Everything her mother wasn't, Victoria was. Only Victoria's tender years, and her mother's hawklike supervision, prevented the scout from being more than a little enthralled by her. She stood a respectful two paces behind her mother in the aisle.

"My daughter has prevailed upon me to allow you to recount another of your marvelously fanciful tales of the frontier," the regal Mrs. York declared.

"Ummm—aaah," Holten delayed.

"Oh, please, Mr. Holten," Victoria appealed. "They are simply the most wonderfully exciting stories I've ever heard. Maybe one about the—the Sioux." She shivered in vicarious horror at the images the tribal name called up. Soft, brown, puppy-dog eyes pleaded her case.

"Haa-ummm. The Sioux, eh? Well, I suppose . . . Excuse me, please take a seat."

"Oh, yes. I can hardly wait until we get to my cousin's house in Abilene. She'll just die with envy for not hearing you yourself," Victoria cooed.

Holten launched into another adventure, full of Indian battles and frontier hardships, and then several more, which kept Victoria fascinated for the better part of the afternoon.

* * *

31

"The way the Boss sees it, those fellers down there are falling trees that are rightfully his," Al Handy advised the band of border ruffians with him. "There's twenty—twenty-five of them in that camp, near three to one. But they're not gunhands. Watch out for their axes, though. Saw a logger throw one thirty feet once and stick it right in the center of a bull's-eye."

"We gonna run 'em off like before?" one of the gang asked.

Handy gave him a wintry grimace that passed for a smile. "Watch and see," the short, stocky gunhawk said. His pale blue eyes grew even more colorless as he drew his Smith & Wesson .44 American. With a nod, he gave the signal to ride down on the logging camp.

A dozen cruisers worked at notching trees for the sawyers to come along and fall with two-man cross-cuts and wedges. Dragline operators, their hands filled with reins from the eight-span mule teams, snaked the trimmed logs down to a stout building a short distance away. Constructed of raw beams and slab cuts, the sturdy structure housed the big, steam-powered band saw. The constant screech of its passage through green wood drowned out the thudding approach of the outlaws.

They drew nearer as a huge, rough-barked giant gave a preliminary shudder. The sawyer glanced up, prepared to shout his usual warning. He caught sight of the grim-faced, heavily armed men riding down on them, weapons ready, and the word "Timber," died in his mouth.

"What the hell?" came out instead, a moment before Al Handy shot him between the eyes.

Men shouted and ran, one cruiser paused long enough to hurl his double-bit axe with stunning accuracy. It struck, edge-on, in the chest of one hardcase. Then gunshots erupted through the timber. Another axe whizzed through the air and landed

32

handle-first against the broad chest of a horse. The surprised rider shot the logger as he turned to run. Now men screamed and died. Others streaked through the trees in search of safety.

"Cut 'em off!" Al Handy yelled at his men. "Don't leave any witnesses."

Exacting a bloody toll, the butchery became terrible. Two pudgy cooks came from the eating shack and fell to their knees, arms raised and hands clasped in supplication. Burt Sands light-footed his mount to within ten feet of the cringing men. He lifted the muzzle of his Winchester and casually shot the larger cook in the chest. The remaining bean burner tried to come to his feet and run.

He nearly made it while Burt levered a fresh cartridge into the chamber. Then his Winchester barked again and shattered a thumb-sized portion of the cook's spine. Paralyzed from the waist down, the unfortunate man flopped on the ground. His upper portion moved in a frenzy while numbness and cold inhabited his lower extremities. Sands eased in closer and bent down, the hot muzzle of rifle behind the cook's right ear.

"*Adios,* sucker," Burt said lightly as he pulled the trigger.

For a while after the attack ended sporadic gunshots announced the dispatching of a wounded man or one who had earlier hidden. Al Handy stood in the dooryard of the cook shack. In one hand he held a large, steaming bowl of excellent stew. The other he used to ply a large spoon, ladling generous bites into his mouth. He chewed contemplatively. Grinning broadly, Burt Sands came up to him.

"Ya know, the next time we do one of these, we ought to make it look like Indians did it."

Al considered that a moment and nodded. Through half a mouthful of stew, he allowed as how that had

33

been a good idea. "I'll take it up with the Boss," he added.

Far from lust on his mind, Eli Holten enjoyed the time he spent with Victoria York as a rare, normal social situation. At his suggestion, and Victoria's insistence, mother and daughter dined with him that evening. The Kansas & Pacific had employed an excellent chef for their premier train. White linen and silver candelabra decorated the tables. Fresh spring flowers in tiny silver vases added color. The service was excellent and constant, without being obsequious.

In uniforms of white jacket and black trousers, the colored waiters never let a water glass get below the halfway line before they swept down on the table to refill. Savory aromas floated out from behind the full-length swinging door to the kitchen. Holten ordered a tureen of turtle soup first. It arrived steaming from under the lid of a white china bowl, crystal clear with a slight greenish cast, bits of succulent meat floating in the broth. In his years on the frontier, Eli had consumed plenty of land tortoises, broiled, roasted, boiled and stewed. None had ever come close to the ambrosial flavor of the chef's green turtle soup. The faint hint of sherry crowned it with excellence.

For the second course, Eli ordered with the ladies in mind: watercress salad. It didn't do much for him, but Mrs. York and Victoria oohed and awed over it. Next came a brace of quail for each, served with rice and black-eyed peas. Fresh-baked bread added a yeasty savor. The main course came at last; a crown rack of lamb ribs, roasted to a rich, glossy brown, accompanied by mint jelly and fresh sprigs of mint. By then, Holten, who ate sparingly at the best of times, felt some distress.

Not so Victoria, who, for all her dainty size and curves, ate like a farmhand. All the while they chatted.

34

Their solicitous waiter noted the pained signs of the over-fed and suggested a wine to Eli Holten, to "settle the stomach." Eli readily agreed.

At last the feast ended with small, individual Black Forest cakes. Eli tended to shun sweets, so he picked indifferently at his. When Victoria scraped up the last crumb of hers, he pushed back his chair with a sigh of relief.

"I think a little stroll for the length of the train and back is in order."

Victoria clapped her hands in immediate enthusiasm. "How perfect! I'll accompany you. Mother," she said, turning to Mrs. York, "why don't you fetch a porter to prepare our berths. Then you can rest after so sumptuous a meal."

Momma York didn't see her daughter's infatuation as natural teenage curiosity. Inwardly she trembled with outrage at what her dear sister would think when they reached Abilene. Perhaps she wouldn't have to mention it, she mused. Brushing a napkin to her shadow of mustache, Mrs York rose.

"I—ah—yes, I suppose that would be best. You won't be long?" she added pointedly.

"No, Mother, of course not," Victoria responded lightly.

Alone with him at last, she exalted. Her sweet, little-girl smile remained until the wide prow of matronly Momma divided the expectant diners waiting for vacant tables at the end of the car. Then she extended a hand to Eli.

"Shall we go? The, ah, other way."

Young, innocent, kind to strangers, Eli Holten catalogued the attributes and virtues of this lovely creature. He answered with a smile and a nod, took her hand and placed it on one arm. They started off for the front of the train. By accident, or perhaps design, Victoria swayed against Eli's left hip with each gentle rock of the cars they passed through. The firm, warm

35

pressure became extremely noticeable to Eli.

Unbidden, his rebellious body became sensitive to each touch. It heated with the continuation, and his loins stirred. *Dammit,* he mentally cursed his awakening desire, *not now. She's a child, a sweet, innocent ch—woman. A lovely, tender, young woman,* his other, unrepentant self reminded. Victoria chattered on as darkness spread westward behind them, conquering the vivid pastel artistry of twilight.

When they reached the locked entrance to the express car, Eli stepped to the vestibule window and directed Victoria's gaze along the length of the train. Yellow rectangles of oil lamp light played on the ground, which rushed by at the spectacular speed of forty-five miles an hour. The sight pleased her, and she gave a little squeak, then rose on tiptoe and planted a light, fleeting peck on Eli's lips.

"I knew train travel would be exciting," she confided. "I've never been away from home before, and I so want it to be an adventure."

"Sometimes adventures can be a bit hazardous. There are people out there, for instance, who think robbing trains is an easy way to make a living."

"You're teasing me," Victoria answered Eli.

"No, I'm not. The chances are better that no one will, but it could happen."

"Oooh—ooh." She shivered. "Let's start back. I heard there is an observation platform on the back of the train. I've never been there. Could we go?" Victoria requested coyly

"I don't see why not," Eli allowed.

Three small children captured Victoria's attention in a chair car. A big-eyed girl had large, silent tears sliding down her cheeks. When Victoria asked lightly what the matter might be, the child sobbed out her fright.

"It moves so much and goes so fast . . . I'm scared."

Victoria cuddled her while two boys chased each other around the small space between the convenience

36

room and one row of seats. Victoria mopped the last of the girl's tears and motioned to them.

"Come here, boys. Now, does the motion of the train frighten you?"

"Naw," the carrot-topped one responded, wrinkling his freckles to make a face.

"Not me," his companion solemnly declared.

"You see?" she pointed out to the unhappy girl. Then, to the boys, she asked, "Why don't you ask her to join your game of tag?"

Two young faces screwed into expressions of agony. "She's a *girl*," the redheaded one bemoaned.

"Yeah," his dark-haired pal acknowledged. "Who wants to play with a girl?"

Her gender at issue, the child in Victoria's lap forgot her fear for the moment to defend herself. "I can run faster than you," she challenged.

"Think so, huh?" the speckle-faced lad taunted. "Betcha can't."

"Oh, yeah?" The angelic lips froze in a pout of contempt.

"Yeah," both boys chorused.

Jumping lightly from Victoria's lap, she squealed in delight. "I'm it, you better run."

Laughing joyously, Victoria rejoined Eli, and they strolled on. At last they came to the final car, a combination smoking car and roomettes. By that time, nearly everyone had retired to their sleeper berths or rooms, the chair car passengers curled up in seats. Only two men sipped brandy and smoked cigars in the smoker end when Eli and Victoria entered. They extinguished their cheroots and spoke mutual good nights at the appearance of the young people. Holten led Victoria to the last door on the train.

The rumble and click of the trucks and the hiss of passing air grew clearer outside on the observation platform. Eli took Victoria by the hand and led her to the protective rail extended some three feet beyond the rear truck. In all directions they could see; not a light broke the velvety darkness of the prairie. Stars provided weak illumination of the foreground, with the milky light of a waxing quarter moon. Holten swept his arm in a wide gesture to encompass all the visible sky.

"I hadn't seen the stars—really *seen* them—until I came west. Then I learned the Sioux names. After that, when I went to work for the army, Frank Corrington took time to teach me their proper names." He paused and chuckled. "Though I'm not sure whose names came first so as to be the *proper* ones."

"What are the Sioux names?" Victoria asked, genuinely interested.

"Look up to your right there. See that constellation that looks like two figures stuck together. That's the Pleiadese. The Sioux call them the Sky Sisters. Up there to the north, to your left, see the Dipper? The Sioux call them *Pta* and *Ptala,* Herd Father and Little Bull."

"That's . . . sort of . . . sweet. Now, do I have to give you a lesson on how to recognize plain, obvious signs?" Victoria asked tauntingly.

"Wha-what are you getting at?"

"Mr. Eli Holten, the very idea. My mother thinks you, like everyone of the male gender, are interested in only one thing—getting into my bloomers. She's terrified that you will steal away my 'pearl of great price' and leave me unsuited for a proper marriage. That's all I've heard from her since we met."

Taken aback, Eli worked his jaw a moment before mustering words. "And what do you think?"

An expression of mischief squeezed Victoria's features. "I think I'd just love it if you got into my bloomers. Or bothered me in some other manner."

"Victoria, ah, you're a mere girl, a young lady not—not quite ripe enough for——" Victoria's hand on his chest arrested his words.

"Oh, I'm ripe enough, all right," she assured the

38

astonishesd scout. "More than you could ever imagine. I—I've wanted to be alone with you since the moment I first saw you."

With a winsome smile, Victoria sank to her knees. Swiftly she began to fumble with the fly of his trousers. Holten gasped and made a croaking sound.

"Don't say anything; don't do anything. Just rest against the door and enjoy."

Warm and soft, the touch of her hand against the sensitive flesh of his semi-erect organ sent a shock through Holten's body. With firm insistence she quickly tugged it free. Then a greater jolt of pleasure surged through him as Victoria closed her mouth over the sensitive tip.

Her tongue dodged and flirted with his rapidly enlarging phallus, sending pulses of delight outward from his groin. Eli dropped a hand to the top of her head, fondling her lush, fine hair. Victoria moaned softly and began to rock back and forth, ingesting more of his manhood with each completed cycle. Oh, how she loved it. Eagerly she licked its great length and slathered the excitable tip with feathery lips. Her hands, no less skilled, did not remain idle. She cupped his contracted sack and kneaded the contents, setting off new spasms of joy.

"My God, Vic-Vickie. You shouldn't—what if—where did . . . ?" Eli blurted while his carnal self reveled in the remarkable performance she put on for him.

Slowly Victoria worked him along the incline toward the abyss of release. Each clever new technique she employed sent Eli higher into the gossamer mists that concealed ultimate completion. When he gasped involuntarily at the onset of climax, she withdrew the substantial part of him from her mouth and waited, head cocked to one side as though counting. Then she took him in again.

Eli's knees felt weak, and he spun in fevered frenzy by the time she at last allowed him to peak and explode into eternity. When his contractions subsided, Victoria tidied herself and him, replaced his powerful engine in his trousers and rose gracefully. Her face beamed with her own spiritual upheaval. She sighed and patted his cheek.

"Uh . . . outside of something hackneyed, like this was so sudden, I don't know what . . . uh, well, ah, it was—was re-remarkable," Holten stammered. "Maybe we can carry this further in my Pullman berth."

"No—no, dear Eli. That can't be. You see, I intend to keep my promise to my mother and save my innocence for the marriage bed. The first man to know me, in the Biblical sense, will be my husband. I've n-never lain with a man. However, I developed rather early," she added with a suppressed giggle. "Quite early, in fact." She moved against him, firm, young breasts pressed to Eli's chest, right at the bottom of his rib cage.

"Not long after I learned how to entertain myself, I discovered that contact with boys was even more pleasurable. I—ah—my mother had been haranguing me since the age of six about how horrible it all was. How, although it was necessary to endure in order to Hold A Man—and she said it in capital letters—to a woman the whole rigamarole was distinctly unpleasant. Her tirade sort of peaked out when I was eight and I promised her faithfully to never have anything to do with, not even thoughts about, men until I had to debase myself in the marriage bed."

"You, ah, you're an only child?" Holten guessed.

Victoria lowered her eyes a moment, then returned her hot gaze to Eli's steely gray orbs. "Yes, I am. Mother and Father have slept in separate rooms for as long as I can remember. But, back to what I was trying to explain. About the same time I promised her that, I developed this overwhelming urge to, ah, experiment. So I did. Within three years I had learned several means of sharing pleasure without making the Ultimate Sacrifice, as Mother put it. Since that time, I've been sharing my secret with a lot of boys and not a few men. I . . . hope you don't think less of me for—for what happened. I really couldn't help myself."

In spite of his reservations, a big grin spread on Eli's face. "You did . . . quite well. Now we had better get back before Mother discovers the Terrible Truth." He had to fight a rich guffaw that rose in his throat. God, one evening with this child of delight and he'd caught her habit of capitalizing words. What would the rest of the journey bring?

CHAPTER 4

It had not been since he was a small child, White Horse thought, that the people had buried anyone there. The thirty-year-old Dog Soldier sat his pony in a rich stand of lodgepole pine and looked toward the sacred hill. Father of three, White Horse had gained considerable respect among the Cheyenne. He had, in fact, spoken against this expedition to determine how badly the whites had despoiled their holy places. Discovery would lead to anger and that to war.

White Horse did not believe any benefit existed for the Cheyenne to war with the whites. They had in the end forced the Big Medicine of the Sioux, Crazy Horse, onto a reservation and there murdered him. A year later they arranged the death of Sitting Bull. If it happened to the mighty Sioux, what could the Cheyenne expect? Now his fine cerebral exercise in restraint flew to the winds as he sat and watched white-eyes yanking down burial scaffolds and trampling among the treasures of the departed.

All they could see was gold, White Horse told himself, but that didn't change the enormity of their sacrilege. He glanced quickly left and right to see his companions and brothers of the Dog Soldier warrior society suffused with anger like himself. They held their weapons ready. The time had come to use them.

"Leave none of them alive," White Horse grunted.

Eager to strip the mantle from Mother Earth and expose the rich deposits of gold they believed lay below, the prospectors and curious idlers cavorted drunkenly and threw shovels of dirt in all directions. The twenty or so despoilers looked up in stunned horror as fifteen painted, heavily armed Cheyenne warriors broke the trees and thundered downslope to the flat-topped knoll where the tribe had buried its noted chiefs for more than three centuries. Howling soul-freezing war cries, the vengeful men from Shutai's band fired a few unaimed rounds while they rapidly closed the distance between them and the suddenly motionless white men.

"My God! Injuns!"

"Those are Cheyenne! Oh, Lord, help us."

Gradually mobility returned to the interlopers. First one, then another began to move, as though knee deep in molasses. One young gold-seeker leaped off the ground in a dive that carried him past two others. He came up with an old Spencer rifle in his hands. As though it had been a signal, a shower of arrows flew from the advancing Cheyenne.

Several struck flesh—one in a grizzled old-timer's left eye socket. He screamed like a wounded horse and abruptly sat on the ground. With both hands he tried to support the shaft and ease his brain-frying agony. The slightest movement worked the vicious projectile deeper into his head. Rifles on both flanks cracked at the beleaguered white men. More arrows fell among them.

Four corpses lay on the ground when the Cheyenne rode in among the defenders. Without pause, the warriors leaped from their mounts, grabbing the offending whites and wrestling them to the ground. Tomahawks and knives did their grisly work. Horrid shrieks came from the dying, for the Cheyenne exercised exquisite cruelty in dispatching their enemy.

The young man who had first seized a rifle blasted one of the attackers into oblivion.

In the next instant, a long, slender flint lance point entered his lower belly and sliced upward, disemboweling him before White Horse yanked it free. Less than three minutes after they attacked, only the Cheyenne stood upright among the burial scaffolds. Three whites still quivered out the last moments of their lives. The mutilations and scalpings began with them.

White Horse let go a mighty whoop. "The white ones will defile this place no more!"

Thirty adults, and a gaggle of a dozen play-minded children, had gathered to commemorate what to them was an auspicious occasion. Working with an aggressive boomer company, the fifteen families who had settled in this western corner of the Black Hills had surveyed and laid out the grid for the streets. A town would soon be established in the pleasant bowllike valley.

"Would you say a few words in blessing of our enterprise, Rev'rend Evers?" a portly gentleman who had ambitions of being mayor requested when the group assembled beside a stake-marked building.

"Yes, Brother Dower. Lord, look kindly upon this gathering, bless their fledgling community with success and help it to prosper. For it is through . . ." the reverend rambled on, until the youngsters squirmed and a number of the less pious men glanced heavenward, wondering if God was getting as bored as they.

"Thank you, Rev'rend," Dower responded when the prayer mercifully ended. "Now, it's with great pleasure that I take up this shovel to turn the first ground on what will be a mighty city in the future. Fortunately the litter of bones has been removed, which will make our task the easier."

While conducting the survey, the team employed

from back East had noted the unusual abundance of large bones and buffalo skulls. Being easterners they paid it no mind. It would have boded far better for everyone had they made some further inquiry into the reason behind this unnatural phenomenon. They would have learned that other tribes besides the Cheyenne and Sioux used portions of the sacred *Hesapa* for the annual Sun Dance.

In this instance, the would-be town builders had selected the site of the Arapaho Sun Dance. They discovered their error shortly after the first clot of dirt had been turned over by the gold-ribbon-decorated shovel. Scattered applause from the ladies and a lusty cheer from the gentlemen ended in shouts of alarm and terror as thirty howling Arapaho warriors appeared over the rim of the valley at a gallop.

Brandishing feather-bedecked lances and war clubs, the braves thundered down the gradual slope and in amongst the startled and thoroughly frightened whites. Children shrieked and ran pell mell in an effort to avoid the flashing hoofs and churning legs of the war ponies. Arrows hummed their eeeire death song and twanged musically when they struck wagon sides or stuck in the hard earth. A few men had the presence of mind to draw their weapons and open fire.

With the introduction of resistance, the aim of the warriors improved markedly. Two men went down with arrows in their shoulders. A horse screamed in agony and ran erratically across the valley floor, blinded by pain. Two small boys and a little girl suddenly left the ground in the strong arms of Arapaho warriors. Their shrieks of alarm turned to howls of pure terror. One lad wriggled and struck with small fists at the bare chest of his captor.

"Leggo me, you ol' fart!" he yelled.

Although the words meant nothing to him, the Arapaho answered in his own tongue, laughing. "You are a brave one, Cricket. You must have something swinging between your legs besides a shriveled worm." The young war chief gestured to his companions who had also scooped up children. "Come. We'll take them for a ride."

So saying, he set off at a gallop for the eastern rim of the valley. The other two warriors followed. It didn't take the whites long to get the implied message. The Indians wanted them out of the valley. The Arapaho made it clear they wanted them gone in the directions from which whites always seemed to come. Gathering their scattered courage, the town builders hastened to wagons, carriages and horses. Harassed on the flanks by the remaining braves, they streamed after the trio who had taken the children. Within thirty minutes the Arapaho Nation secured sole possession of their Sun Dance ground.

"It's the Reverend Sommers, sir," Sergeant Major Childers of the 12th announced when he opened the door.

Lieutenant Colonel Mayberry glanced up from the onerous task of reading the supply survey and nodded. "Send him in, Sergeant Major."

"Yes, sir."

Hershel Sommers, who looked forty-five and claimed to sixty-four years old, entered. His thick, salt-and-pepper hair resembled the shaggy, unkempt mane of a regal lion. A boyish smile illuminated his youthful face, devoid of hair decoration. He extended a large, squarish hand to the cavalry officer as he strode across the floor.

"It's good you would see me on so short notice, Colonel."

"You take me away from an unpleasant task, Reverend, so I'll not begrudge the time. What brings you to Fort Rawlins?"

Reverend Sommers frowned and accepted the chair

46

Lieutenant Colonel Mayberry indicated. "Some rather disturbing evidence that recently came into my possession, Colonel."

"Please, call me Howard. Military protocol has no standing among civilians, or the clergy."

"Very well, ah, Howard. My Christian name is Hershel. I'm afraid that this time I don't come as a herald of the Lord," he said lightly, referring to the origin of his name. "Rather, as a harbinger of ill tidings."

"How's that? You've made that most obvious and, I might say, piqued my curiosity, Hershel."

"That's because . . . I hesitate to make such an accusation, but I must."

"Are some of my troops in trouble with the agency?" Mayberry prodded.

"No—no, nothing of the sort. What I have uncovered is definite proof that the territorial government is . . . the government is deliberately siding with the land thieves and murderers who have invaded the Black Hills." The cleric assumed a "there, I've said it" expression.

Electrified by the possibilities this opened, Lieutenant Colonel Mayberry intently studied his visitor. His words were couched in a tone nearing incredulity. "You're certain of this? Do you actually believe the governor and others in the territorial government capable of such a thing?"

Reverend Sommers didn't even hesitate. "I consider the politicians—I dare say *all* politicians—no less corrupt than the worst of the invading horde of prospectors, sharpers and loose women. Their conduct in office so far has been less than laudatory. I understand from friends in Pierre that scandal and hints of corruption are so rampant that no one of honest mean takes our good governor seriously. More to the point, I have also learned that the tribes are not taking this invasion calmly.

"The Cheyenne and Arapaho have sent emissaries to Pine Ridge and the other Sioux agencies. They talk of war. Already the Cheyenne and Arapaho have taken action against those who have defiled sacred places in the Black Hills. To my surprise, the army has done nothing."

"Department Headquarters has agreed to consider this a civil dispute, under the jurisdiction of the territorial government. We have been ordered not to take an active role in the solution of any problems." His words tasted of the sour bile of embarrassment and outrage.

"Meanwhile the tribes are working themselves up into a full-scale uprising. Will the governor and his cronies provide protection when that happens?"

Mayberry chuckled, a cynical chortle. "Oh, I'm quite certain that when the situation becomes sufficiently explosive, Governor Stratton will bleat and whine for the army's intervention to curb the hostiles. When it suits his purpose. Now I have a question for you."

"Go ahead, Howard."

"Do you know of any of your charges who might hold enough of a grudge against General Corrington to attack and savagely beat him, then leave him for dead on the prairie?"

Hershel Sommers contemplated a long span. "I—ah—I'm not sure. Granted, every Sioux can rightfully claim some rancor toward the general. Yet, that's not like them."

"Meaning?"

"If the Sioux had done something like that, they'd have made sure he was dead. To return to our earlier topic, I am anxious to discover what, if anything, can be done to prevent an all-out Indian war. I've written my superiors; they tend to pontificate and not listen to advice from such unqualified persons as those actually in the field. So, if this situation continues, I'd like to know what Washington will do about it?"

"Nothing," Howard Mayberry snapped. Then he amended, "Provided we can't prove to their satisfaction that Governor Stratton and his fellow politicians are directly involved in a deliberate provocation of the Indians."

"I have that proof. I've sent affidavits to BIA and the Interior Department. I'm afraid that's about as productive as spitting into the wind. Unless and until someone pays attention to that proof, I'm afraid the Center of the World, as the Sioux call the Black Hills, is about to explode into a bloody confrontation. I've been here enough years to know that only the army can stand between the white plunderers and the angry Indians."

"And, with General Corrington lying in a coma, that means Eli Holten," the colonel said almost prayerfully.

"Holten? I've heard of him, of course, but what makes him so important?" Reverend Sommers asked.

"Do you have some time? Well, then, I'll tell you."

Their parting had been memorable. The Daylight Express pulled into Abilene, Kansas at seven-forty-five in the morning. There would be an hour layover before it departed for the completion of its run. While Mrs. York went officiously to supervise the off-loading of their voluminous luggage, Vicki and Eli Holten strolled along the depot platform. They had enjoyed three memorable sessions during the trip, all ending with Vicki's virtue at least physically intact. Vicki found a small, empty room and darted into it. She tugged Eli along with one hand.

"Oh, Eli, you are the most wonderful man I've ever known," she gushed breathlessly after closing the door. "I just wish that—that it could be you who—who—" Vicki lowered her eyes and brought a pink blush to her creamy cheeks—"who claimed my prize. But we still have time for . . ." Suiting her actions to her words, she

49

sank to a small bench and undid Eli's fly.

"Uh—Vicki. Don't you think . . ." Eli began. Then his resistance melted when her soft, moist fingers closed around the partially risen shaft of his organ.

Her lips, soft and busy as a humming bird's wings, played across the sensitive tip of Eli's rapidly swelling member. She gasped and moaned and began to lick. Eli had never met a woman so dedicated to that particular erotic performance and, not for the first time, wondered if she was entirely normal. Her warm, silken lips soon dispelled any concern. Vicki employed fantastic talent to swiftly elevate Eli to a state of euphoria.

"Oh, Eli—" she broke off to gasp—"I can't get enough of you a-and there's so much of you to get."

Holten almost lost it then. The overwhelming urge to laugh, to at least guffaw uproariously, teased the corners of his mouth, full lips twitching in anticipation. Vicki returned to her task. The insistant tugging of her energetic efforts drew a moan of appreciation from Eli. Searching his memories, he could not recall saying good-bye in quite this manner before. Vicki's arousal brought forth groans and grunts and the smack of talented lips.

"Easy, kid, easy," Eli urged as her loving grew more urgent. "Aaah—oh—yeah. We—we'd better stop," he suggested. "Your moth—"

Vicki paused in her herculean endeavor. "Mother doesn't know any more about real loving than she does about building a house. Don't talk, Eli, just enjoy. It's—it's our l-last time." Tears added new highlights to her eyes.

Holten put a hand to her head, stroking the silken hair, as he basked in the warmth that radiated from his loins. Expertly, Vicki led him to the edge of oblivion, hesitated while his body and emotions subsided, then again, and again, and yet another time before joyfully sending him over the invisible barrier into a protracted moment of sheer dissolution.

When she had restored Eli to propriety, Vicki hugged him mightily, graceful, well-turned arms tightly squeezing his chest while she ground her pelvis against his pubic crest. Her eyes shined when their embrace ended.

"I'll never, never forget you, Eli. Now, good-bye, good-bye. Don't watch after me while I fade from your life forever, beloved."

In a swirl of skirts she was gone. Eli Holten felt faintly embarrassed by her maudlin, romantic notions. He also felt superbly drained. If nothing else came along until he could return to Concha and Cherry, he could manage quite well. Sudden images of Gen. Frank Corrington lying severely injured in a hospital bed drove all frivolity from Eli's thoughts. He still had so far to go.

CHAPTER 5

Big driver wheel weights flashing in the sun, the American Locomotive Works 4-6-2 gained speed as it leaned into the slight upgrade eastward out of Abilene, Kansas. Smoke boiled from a fat column, round and black on top like a huge mushroom steam-laced with gray through the stem. The click-clack of the trucks over rail joints decreased in interval as the swaying of the cars smoothed out and grew constant. It brought to Holten's mind warm memories of his long, friendly relationship with Frank Corrington.

"Brandy, Eli? take a cigar." Gen. Frank Corrington invariably began meetings with his chief scout that way whenever the job Holten would be sent on promised to be a dirty one.

Dirty and dangerous. General Corrington saw that Eli Holten got them all. If inclined to be romantic, which Eli considered himself definitely not to be, he might describe them as wild adventures. There had been the Carter brothers, who sold bad whiskey and poor quality rifles to the Indians. By themselves, they represented more an irritant than a risk. Yet they opened a can of particularly nasty worms that nearly got Eli Holten killed in the bargain.

Or consider the uprising of Two Bulls. A British subject with a yen for his own empire had brought death and destruction to the prairie, until Frank Corrington sent Eli Holten to wipe out the sin city guarded by deadly Parrot rifles. With the corrupt town in flames and the Sioux riding for once as allies to the cavalry, Two Bulls had returned to peaceful ways. Then there was the expedition with Nelson Miles to put the Sioux on reservations. Mercifully, he had not been attached by headquarters to the Seventh in that fateful summer of '76. Frank Corrington knew of, and shared, Eli Holten's contempt for George Armstrong Custer. The second expedition with Miles had not been so pleasant.

Chief Joseph of the Nez Percé had been hounded, harried and humiliated, his people devastated. Eli Holten had returned from the moving, emotional surrender in time to witness the cold, callous murder of Crazy Horse. There had always been "just one more mean one, Eli."

Now the tough, determined soldier who had risen from a green shave-tail at First Manassas to CO of the 12th U.S. Cavalry and on to commanding general of the garrison at Fort Rawlins lay on the edge of death in the dispensery at that same fort. Deep, sincere emotional pain twisted in Holten's gut. Who could have done it, and why? Those questions, the scout vowed, would soon be answered when he got to Fort Rawlins. Abandoning unproductive speculation, Holten pulled down on the front brim of his hat and closed shaded eyes for a mid-morning nap.

Awakened refreshed, Eli had a solitary, though satisfactory, noon meal and strolled to the smoking car to enjoy one of the long, thin cigars he favored. For all the unreality of their brief relationship, Holten had to admit he already missed litte Vicki. While he worked at perfecting his smoke rings, Eli returned to images of the past. His reflections ended when the train came to a halt in the tortured screech of metal on metal. Curious, Holten did something about it, unlike other passengers, who remained anxiously wondering in their seats.

His boot soles hit the gravel track ballast after a short jump from the bottom vestibule step. From ahead he could see a black column of smoke rising lazily into the blue Kansas sky. He observed members of the train crew hurrying forward. Abandoning the slanted rock pile, he made quick time catching up to them.

A forty foot gorge described the course of the Neosho River. Several supports of the trestle that spanned it now burned cheerily. By the time Holten arrived at a vantage point, crewmen already heaved buckets of water from the snowmelt swollen river against the burning pilings. Their voices floated up like sparrow chirps.

"Ga-dang, weren't no accident, I tell you," the conductor declared.

"Deke's right," one brakeman agreed. "No hotbox set this off. Too far down, and look there. Someone piled straw bales against the pilings."

"Why'd they do a thing like that?" the switchman asked.

Deke, the conductor, looked around suspiciously. "I got a feeling we'll find out 'fore long."

Holten thought to offer his assistance, then realized the fire would be out before he could descend to the bottom of the river gorge. Assaulted by shovels of dirt and buckets of water, the last flame died in less than ten minutes. What would take longer, Eli surmised, was testing the trestle to insure it was strong enough to hold the train. Three brakemen remained to test the charred pilings with spike hammers, slamming them with powerful blows and listening to the musical resonance of the wood. The switchmen climbed toward where Holten stood.

"Might as well stretch your legs," the first one suggested to him. "This is gonna take a while."

They broke the coupling between the locomotive

tender and the express car, and the engineer eased out onto the bridge. The drivers spun, hissing in the sand discharged for traction. Inches at a time the heavy steam engine rolled out onto the fragile-looking construction. At that pace the creak and groan of the wood could be clearly heard. For a giddy moment, Holten considered that if it sounded that loud at normal speed, no one would ever ride the trains.

When the full weight of the locomotive and wood-filled tender bore on the damaged pilings without breaking any, the engineer gave four short hoots on the steam whistle and began to back up. A sudden movement at a fold in the limestone hills attracted Eli Holten's attention. The coupler knuckles had barely slammed together to reconnect the train when a dozen masked men rode down on the cars.

Weapons blazed and sent gawking passengers scurrying. Holten had a hand wrapped around the butt grips of his Remington in an instant. A bullet broke glass in one coach window, and Eli triggered a round. Before the outlaws could reach the stalled train, Eli ran to the nearest passenger car and bounded aboard.

"All right, any of you with firearms, get on the left side of the car, at a window. Pick an outlaw and start shooting." He started for the back of the coach.

"Where are you going?" a portly man with a small pocket pistol demanded.

"To get some more people organized," Holten snapped.

On the vestibule, he paused long enough to take careful aim and blow a robber out of his saddle. Feminine squeaks of alarm, followed by anxious questions, greeted him in the next car. Holten wasted no time.

"If you've got a gun, use it. The train is being robbed. About a dozen men out there. Half of you on the left, half to the right. They'll try to circle around."

Gaping mouths and blank stares greeted him. It

came to Holten that with his old slouch trail hat and a sixgun in his hand he must look very like a bandit himself. He removed the battered brown hat and sailed it toward an empty seat.

"Don't just stand there. You're going to have to defend yourselves."

"But, the railroad—"

Holten's glower withered the chubby, moon-faced man and cut off his protest. "Is busy enough trying to defend the express car. If you haven't any stomach for defending yourself, you might as well go out there and give up to the bandits."

Breaking glass and gunshots satisfied the scout that some of the men had taken heart. He moved on to the next coach. There someone else had organized the men, and they engaged the enemy outside with determination. The dining car came next, and Eli found it a shambles. Broken glass lay on most tables, with overturned cups and glasses, a smashed sugar bowl, two completely befuddled and frightened late diners, and the six white-jacketed, colored waiters, their eyes rolling like huge white marbles with black dots. A bullet punched through glass in the end door and whined off the brass rail at the buffet bar.

Eli Holten had instinctively dodged to one side and instantly loosed a round in response. A soft grunt came from beyond the damaged wooden panel. It swung open the next instant, and a masked man stumbled into the car on rubbery legs. He tried to raise a .45 Colt revolver, found it unaccountably too heavy and released the sixgun with a tired sigh. His body followed it to the floor at once. Holten stepped over the dead man and started for the vestibule.

"Oh, Lordy, ain't you gonna stay an' protec' us?" one of the waiters wailed.

"Take that outlaw's gun and protect yourself," Holten snapped as he disappeared out the door.

A rapid rattle of gunfire from behind him, punctuated by the flat boom of a 10 gauge shotgun, announced the outlaws' attempt on the express car. Instinct urged Holten to head that direction. Caution, and the lack of supportive fire, argued for his present course. A shrill feminine scream assured him of the wisdom of his decision.

He came upon the three of them on the next vestibule. The woman the trio held on to was young, a girl really, not more than fifteen. Her face, twisted now in terror and revulsion, would normally be quite beautiful. Her eyes held an expression of wounded innocence. One of the bandits had a hand under her voluminous skirt, hoisting it upward.

"Let her go," Eli Holten said softly, without realizing he had spoken. His words held a purr of menace.

"What th' hell you thin—" the chubby one fumbling with his fly growled as he whirled around.

His snarling voice cut off abruptly when Eli Holten shot him through his open mouth. A saucer-sized disc of his skull slapped his nearest companion on the cheek. Only the train robber on the girl's right possessed wit enough to react promptly. He triggered a round that cracked past Holten's head and rang piercingly off the metal facing of the door frame. Holten's Remington roared again, and the hardcase doubled over, one hand clasped to the belly wound.

Holten swung the muzzle of his sixgun toward the remaining bandit, who decided to dive off the train. Weapon still in hand, Holten stepped close to the girl. Her eyes shifted rapidly in their sockets, like caged wild animals.

"It's all right, miss," Holten began.

"A-all that blood," she croaked. "It just gushed and gushed."

"Let me take you back to your folks," Eli offered, conscious of her shock.

"I—I'm traveling alone."

Eli frowned. "Well then, do you know how to use

57

one of these?" he asked, retrieving one of the outlaws' revolvers.

"I can shoot."

"Good girl. Take this and keep it ready. Don't let them get that close to you again."

"Where are you . . . going?"

"To help some other folks," Holten said curtly.

So far no dynamite had gone off, Eli noted with relief. That meant the robbers had not breached the express car as yet. He forged on toward the rear of the train. Confused men and hysterical women impeded his progress in each coach. When he reached the last, a Pullman observation car, the fighting had ended, except for around the forward end of the train. In his wake, Eli discovered a dozen armed passengers. Quickly he formulated an idea.

"You men come with me. We'll go down the blind side of the train and hit them from where they won't expect it."

On the way along the side of the fifteen-car Daylight Express, Eli Holten vividly recalled the time when his life hung in terrible jeopardy, not from something he had done or was doing, but for something he had no part of at all. Owen Broadbent, an exact look-alike as Eli Holten, ran a gang in Kansas, identifying himself as Eli Holten, robbing banks and trains, murdering indiscriminately. The good people of Kansas nearly hanged the real Eli Holten for Broadbent's crimes. He had, at last, written an epitaph for Owen Broadbent, though not before a great deal of travail.

"There's one of 'em up there," a volunteer's voice drew Eli from his reflections.

Eli looked toward the roof of the livestock car, immediately behind the express coach. One bandit crouched there, his eyes fixed on the end door of the express and mail car. Holten motioned for some of the men to stretch out on the ballast, ready to fire under the train. Others he gave whispered instructions to get between cars and be ready to attack from there. Then he raised his Remington .44 and put a shot into the right shoulder of the man atop the stock car. At once the revenge-hungry passengers opened up.

"Oh, shit! Where'd they come from?" one bandit blurted.

"Don't know, but let's get outta here," another yelled.

Horses whinnied in alarm, and hoofs pounded as the aroused passengers ran and fired. They broke into the open and converged on the laggard two outlaws. Before Holten could stop them, sixguns spoke, and the bandits died of a dozen bullet wounds each. In the silence that followed, one man's voice nearly caused Eli Holten to burst out in a howl of laughter.

"Shit! Oh, shit. One of them shot off the tip of my little finger."

"I still don't see why we have to take the risk of exposing ourselves like this," Hez Manning complained.

"Because if we do not," Amos Wade told him patiently, like an exasperated parent with a slow-witted child, "we'll never be able to depend upon this rabble to follow our orders when we're not around. They may not be overly bright, but they are mean as hell and will feel we can be trusted if we share in some of the killing at the outset."

"That's one damned cold way of explaining it," Zack Walters remarked.

Amos Wade ran thick, stubby fingers through the thinning fringe of gray-black hair that formed a monk's tonsure on his balding head. "Prison, my dear friend Zacharia, tends to abrade one's sensibilities. There'll be time for playing the genteel rich *after* we milk this country for everything we can get. For now, content yourself with the fact we have twenty-five ruthless men with no more conscience than a stone, willing to exercise their hatred of our red-skinned brothers as and where we direct."

"And tonight it's to be the Cheyenne's turn," Hez Manning summed up.

"Well put," Wade praised. "By tomorrow, the Black Hills will be aswarm with blood-lusting savages. Our friend, the governor, will activate the militia, which we shall organize and command. We will sweep the Dakotas clean of hostile Indians, and soon we will have vast holdings which can be milked for a fortune when sold to new pilgrims from back East. Whereupon they shall purchase equipment, tools, supplies and food from our stores, drink and gamble in our saloons, spend their lust in our bordellos, educate their children in our schools, travel our railroads, and form their opinions by reading our newspapers. In other words, we shall own them body and soul."

"Why don't we let the army do the bleeding and dying for us?" Zack Walters protested.

Wade gave him a patronizing flicker of smile. "Because the army is often wont to ask embarrassing, and highly accurate, questions and bring up sticky subjects like treaties. Governor Stratton wants to see a mountain of gold amassed behind his house and so should we. If the army does the fighting for us, then the only ones to benefit will be the failures, malcontents and peasants who flock westward in hopes of 'starting over again.'"

"We can still milk them of everything they have," Zack suggested.

"Only slowly, and in increments. By claiming the land ourselves, selling it and foreclosing on mortgages at opportune times, we'll have it to sell over and over again. Enough of this. We have only a mile or so before we reach the Cheyenne village."

Hez Manning snickered. "I feel a little like Custer at the Washita."

"Better Colonel Chivington," Wade offered. "He lived through Sand Creek. Custer answered the call to glory once too often."

They rode on in silence for a while. Then Manning touched on a subject of equal importance to the trio. "What about the men sent to finish Corrington?"

"No word as yet," Amos Wade responded, turning his cold, hard brown eyes on his companions. "We'll probably hear when we get back to Pierre."

"They had better do it right this time," Zack Walters growled, his thin, cruel lips drawn tightly, an unholy fire in his close-set, icy eyes.

"Time to dismount," Wade advised. "We'll walk the horses from here. We've a good two hours to false dawn. That's when we'll attack."

"Catch them red niggers in their buffalo robes," a subordinate leader in the gang observed from nearby. "Wonder if they'll be humpin' their squaws?"

"More than likely," Zack Walters agreed. "Redskins are horny bastards. I know a feller who rode with Chivington at Sand Creek. He said they turned over one tipi, and there was a couple of little Injun kids in there. Ten an' twelve, maybe. The attack caught them floggin' their logs."

"Don't be disgusting, Zack," Amos Wade complained.

Offended, Walters put a defensive whine in his voice. "He swears it's true. Said li'l Injun boys start early. Must, too. I never even knew about it until I was thirteen."

"A severe case of infantile retardation," Amos Wade said sarcastically.

"Wha-a-aa?"

"Never mind. Over that next ridge, then we wait for the right time."

CHAPTER 6

Not even night birds challenged the still, damp calm of predawn. Insects had long since gone to their rest. The chill air had even sent the usual huge, voracious mosquitos to seek out warmth until day returned. Rabbit Nose and Otter Belly were huddled together, sleeping under a thick Hudson's Bay trade blanket while Šta'a-śi, Seventh Son, took his final turn riding watch on the herd, astride his bareback pony.

From their giggles, Šta'a-śi knew his friends had been into some mischief before they fell asleep. He sighed. For once he regretted having the privilege of last turn at guard, which let him watch the Sun-Father return to awaken the land. He longed to be snuggled under the warm blanket, making mischief with his friends. What had they planned?

Otter Belly had a little brother they all hated. White Owl was always naughty, selfish, and spoiled rotten by Otter Belly's father and older brother. White Owl had a rasping, irritating laugh, which he used often to sneer at the older boys when a bowstring broke or a precious arrow point shattered against stone. Did they plot to smear his upper lip with dog dung while he slept so that he would go around smelling it until he went to the creek to bathe? Or tie a rawhide thong around White Own's penis and fix it to a stake in the ground, then yell fire in the lodge? They would all get a big laugh out of what happened then. Maybe their gleeful conspiracy had to do with—with *girls?*

Bright Star always wanted to play with the boys, not do the things girls were supposed to do. Maybe they would tie her braids together and then around a fat puppy by a strip of rawhide, then frighten the puppy and set it running. What fun. If only he could have been in on the planning. Śta'a-śi jerked the single rein and halted his pony. He had seen something, far across the herd, in the trees along the creek.

Śta'a-śi turned Lightning, his favorite of three ponies, and trotted back toward his sleeping friends. For a boy of eleven summers, he was rich indeed to have three ponies—one a handsome, sturdy-limbed hunting horse. In a few summers, after his dreaming time and the Sun Dance, he would have a sleek, powerful war pony; his father had promised it to him. A flicker of light on pale faces along the creek alarmed him further, and Śta'a-śi drummed bare heels into Lightning's ribs.

"Rabbit Nose, Otter, wake up. There's someone over—" Śta'a-śi spoke low and urgently.

A line of bright orange-yellow flashes stopped the words in his throat. Two seconds later the crackle of gunfire reached Śta'a-śi's ears. His eyes grew wide and round, showing a lot of white. He slid from Lightning's back and shook Otter Belly by one bare shoulder.

"Wake up, we're being attacked," he shouted, the need for silence no longer necessary.

With Al Handy in the lead, the collection of frontier riffraff, half-drunken out of work miners and drifting gunfighters charged the village. In the van rode Amos Wade and Zack Walters. Hezakiah Manning followed with the second wave—the one that would deal with women and children, once the warriors had been neutralized. That better suited Hez's personality, Amos considered.

Hezekiah Manning *liked* hurting women and children. Younger than his two partners, in his mid-forties, Hez had revealed a particularly sadistic streak while incarcerated at the territorial prison in St. Paul. He made life unbearable for the younger inmates, boys of no more than fourteen or fifteen. Although in his full vigor, despite poor food, hard labor and frightening conditions in the prison, Hez lacked the outright aggressiveness of other men. He had become furtive and secretive. Zack Walters, on the other hand, came out of prison with different goals.

In the months since his release, he had honed his former skill with firearms until he became lightning fast and dead-eye accurate with a gun. In achieving that proficiency, he adapted his gunfighting tactics to the new .41 Colt Lightning double-action revolver. It gave Amos Wade comfort simply to have Zack Walters close at hand. Zack also favored a side-by-side 10 gauge Parker shotgun, which he had cut down to twenty-inch barrel-length. He held it ready in one hand as they closed in on the sleeping Cheyenne village. A bright band of white split earth and sky apart to the east and momentarily lightened the view ahead for Amos.

Three startled, Indian faces appeared out of the gloom. One, with roundly open mouth, shouted something unheard over the rumble of pounding hoofs. The other two resolved into bodies with arms raising weapons before the false dawn faded. In that brief moment, Zack's Parker blasted open the early morning, and a column of shot wiped away the face of the shouting Cheyenne. All along the line now, rifles and sixguns spoke a deadly tattoo.

Holes appeared in the conical lodges; bullets found horses, dogs and men. Indian women screamed in fear and anger. Within the beleaguered tipis, the men and older boys snatched up bows or firearms, here and there a lance. They went out into the coming daylight to be shot down with merciless precision.

"It is the white men!" the camp crier shouted. "White men have come among us. To your horses, hurry, drive off the white men."

At the horse herd, three small boys stared in big-eyed wonder. Fear, until now an unknown entity, gnawed at their bellies. Šta'a-ši clutched his light rabbit bow and fumbled with trembling fingers to nock an arrow. Rabbit Nose whimpered without knowing it. Otter Belly involuntarily wet his breechcloth but fingered his knife in anticipation.

"They will come for the horses," Šta'a-ši said quietly. "We must be ready."

"Will they kill us?" Rabbit Nose asked quaveringly.

"Who knows? This is but a day," Šta'a-ši observed. "A good day to die. We will fight them. Go over there, Rabbit. You, Otter, to my right. We will hide and wait until the whites come close. Use your bows well. Shoot for the big parts, their bellies, chests. Put arrows in their ponies."

"I'm afraid," Rabbit Nose protested.

"So am I," Šta'a-ši advised him. "We are herd guards; it is our job to save the ponies."

"Over here, Mart," a white voice called from much closer than Šta'a-ši anticipated. "I found their horses."

"Watch out, they'll have guards," Mart cautioned.

A snort of disgust answered the wary mart. "Li'l bitty boys most like."

Three "li'l bitty boys" launched a trio of arrows as the steady strawberry glow of coming dawn made silhouettes of the invaders. The shafts flew in a slight arc toward the targets. Tricky lighting and nervousness affected the aim somewhat. A band of dark orange joined the color array in the east, fading the dark red to pastel pink. Unseen by the white marauders, the missiles struck home.

A horse screamed and began to rear. It bounded away bearing its helpless rider, pain tormenting the animal. The other two didn't fare so well.

"Ow—dammit! I got stuck in the leg," Mart shouted.

"Ga-gawd, I'm gut-shot, fellers. Oh, God, help me."

By then, three more arrows sought their marks. Mart spotted Šta'a-ši standing tall, slim and brave, drawing his bowstring a third time. Muzzle bloom lighted the scene. The bullet kicked up dirt at the boy's feet, which caused him to release his feathered shaft without a proper target. Mart fired again, and Šta'a-ši crumpled to the ground, a fatal slug in his thin, young breast.

Mart yelled in triumph and looked to his left. His companion uttered a soft groan and slumped forward, the head of an arrow protruding from his back, its fletchings tight against his chest. Cursing blackly, Mart blazed away at his unseen enemy. The fusilade had little effect until four more raiders joined him.

Swiftly they hunted down the courageous youngsters who had routed the first attempt to scatter the herd. The two Cheyenne boys died screaming in a crash of revolver fire. Immediately the horses began to run. Howling with glee, the white invaders streamed after them. Elsewhere in the village, lodges had begun to burn; several had been tipped over. Dead and dying Cheyenne Warriors lay scattered through the spaces between tipis.

"Don't let a one of them get away," Al Handy shouted to his followers.

A young woman, a baby on the cradle board on her back, ran shrieking from two bristle-faced attackers. She tripped over the leg of a dead boy and stumbled forward off balance. Her mishap enabled one of the unemployed miners to catch her. He bashed the baby's skull with the butt of his sixgun and wrenched the cradle board from the horrified mother's back. Then he ripped open the front of her buckskin dress.

While he completed the task of stripping her, his

66

companion joined him, fumbling at his fly. "Me first, Billy. I got my pecker out."

"Hell with you, I'm the one who caught her. Hold her, Ned, while I get a little pokey-pokey."

Ned aided his friend at once. Roughly he threw the young mother to the ground and sat down behind her. He locked his legs around her slender figure, right below her firm, teenaged breasts. Her writhing attempts to resist rape wildly stimulated Ned's keenly sensitive phallus.

"Save some for me, Billy," he cheered on his companion.

"One good thing about it, Ned. You sure can't wear it out," Billy chortled and made answer.

Elsewhere other Cheyenne women and older girls shared the young mother's humiliation and degradation. Blood lust abounded, now made carnal. Here and there a rattle of gunfire or single shots marked the waning resistance, or tragically the death of a child or a wounded brave.

"Whoo-ieeee! I got me a good one. She shore can wiggle."

"Use your eyes, stupid. That ain't no little girl," another marauder admonished.

"Makes no never mind," the rapist returned philosophically. "It's good and tight and wrigglin' around like a trout outta water."

"Ummmm-ummm," another raider injected. "I think I got 'is li'l sister. Right prime meat at that."

"You're both disgusting," a voice declared from a short distance away. "Can't neither one of them be a day over ni—"

His voice cut off as a metal-tipped arrow slid through his larynx and poked out the back of his neck. Gagging, the hardcase sank to his knees, both hands clutched around the red-painted shaft. Cold, heartless laughter reached him.

"That'll learn ya," one of the child rapists guffawed.

67

"Shoulda been down here humpin', instead of up there moralizing."

Swiftly the same brave who had shot the arrow came from hiding and knelt beside the amused rapist. The murdering white didn't think it so funny when the scowling Cheyenne slit his throat. Immediately a pair of gunshots announced the demise of the anguished Cheyenne father. Shouting, several of the killers broke out whiskey flasks from their saddlebags. The burning and destruction went on.

Well into midday, drunk on victory and whiskey, the murderers left the village in flames to ride off and continue their celebration.

Carefully tethered in iron bands and chain, the captive dragon sat on the water and hissed steam. As usual, a crowd gathered on the dock at St. Joseph, Missouri to greet the steam packet. The crew labored to take on fuel and clean, fresh water for the boiler. Others off-loaded cargo in preparation for taking on bales, bundles and crates destined for ports of call far up the Missouri River. On the fringe of the crowd, seeking to make his way to the ticket office, Eli Holten pushed against the stubborn resistance of the gawkers.

"Fixin' to buy a ticket, mister?" chirped a rosy-cheeked waif of ten or so at Eli Holten's right elbow.

His face was dirty, smeared with dust and black axle grease, and mud—not yet dry—had oozed between his bare toes. He had little about him to recommend reliability. Then Holten looked at his clear, candid blue eyes, alight with intelligence and innocence. His winsome smile veritably spoke of integrity.

"Why, yes," Holten responded.

"I can get through here easier than you can. Gimme the money an' tell me where, an' I'll bring your ticket to you. Ah, for half a dollar."

Holten considered the proposition. "You've got a deal. I'm going to Pierre, Dakota Territory."

"Stay here, I'll be right back."

"Hold it! You forgot the money."

"Oh—ah, yeah." The lad took the folded bills and disappeared into the crowd.

At the worst, he would be out the money. Holten speculated. If the boy turned out to be a good kid, instead of a drifter, he might even get his ticket. Now, why in hell had he even taken that risk? At once his subconscious presented images of Sarah-Jane and Michael Clemmer. Michael's big, trusting blue eyes. Yeah, the kid had 'em too.

Damn! Getting soft in the head, Eli chided himself. Then he produced visions of the terrors the Clemmer children had faced, their absolute faith in his ability to rescue them from every travail, the harsh faces of the Comancheros and the fat, bloated, obscene face of Lane Stafford. Past turmoils vanished with a persistent tugging on his left hand.

Holten looked down to find the black-haired waif. "I got your ticket, mister. You got two dollars six bits comin' back. That'll be fifty cents."

"I—ah . . ." Holten had calculated his change also and reached the same figure. "Do you have family around here? Where are your parents?"

The lad lowered his gaze to his bare toes. "M'folks are dead."

"Where do you live?" Holten persisted.

"U-under the wharf."

Holten worked his face, warring with his unexplainable upsurge of emotion. "Keep the change. Buy yourself a pair of shoes and a coat."

"Why? Winter won't come for six or seven months."

Practicality of the most basic sort. Holten felt a pang, remembering his own, similar poverty and what he had suffered before finding a way out of it.

Big, sapphire eyes looked unblinkingly up at him. Eli worked his shoulders as though sifting a heavy load. He dug into his trouser pocket for the small, leather poke.

"You hungry, kid?" he asked.

"Sure. I'm . . . always hungry."

He handed the boy a five dollar gold piece. "Take this to buy food with. You can still keep the change."

The waif shot him a sly look from under long, up-curled lashes. "Gee, mister, why are you doin' all this for me? You, ah . . . want something?"

"No, I—" Then the realization of what the child implied struck him. "Hell no. Goddamned 'civilization' breeds that sort of thing. Just say I know another little boy who might have gone wrong at your age if someone hadn't helped him out. Now get outta here before I boot you in the tail."

"You, ah, want your ticket?"

"Oh—yeah."

Holten grabbed it from the boy's hand and turned away. For a while he wondered at why he had to brush a long, callused finger at the corner of both eyes. Then something else commanded his entire attention—there, among the expectant passengers waiting to board.

She was a vision of loveliness. A fantastic looker with the face of an angel. No, not an angel, but a pixie child, bearing the marks of great, worldly knowledge beyond her years. Eli Holten felt a familiar stirring and instantly forgot the child who had been and the one who had touched that tender spot so well hidden deep within him. The steam whistle on the tall, black, forward stack shrilled, and the throng surged forward.

During the ordeal of moving fitfully along like cattle through a loading chute, the scout kept his eyes on the beautiful young woman some ten people ahead of him in the line. Already it appeared the long trip up the

70

Missouri would be nowhere near so boring as he had anticipated. When the passage steward took her ticket, Holten made note of the name he spoke.

Cynthia. Cynthia Gregory. *Miss* Cynthia Gregory. Eli Holten promised himself that he would have reason to remember it.

CHAPTER 7

Muted thrashing of the water driven over the sidewheel paddles provided a backdrop to the piano music in the main lounge of the *American Eagle* as it labored up the Missouri River. Eli Holten, hat in hand, walked over to a white linen draped table and spoke softly, with all the gallantry he could muster.

"I noticed that you are dining alone. Forgive my forwardness, but I, too, am alone. Might I join you, Miss Gregory?"

She started slightly, which Eli thought made her even more beautiful. "You know my name?"

"Yes. Quite shameless of me. I overheard it when you boarded. Now, please? It isn't right that an attractive young lady like yourself sit alone, without some escort."

Cynthia Gregory dimpled, the indentations in her cheeks coloring pinkly. When she spoke, a slight Southern accent became more pronounced. "Why, how could a lady refuse such gallantry. Please be seated, Mister . . . ?"

"Holten. Eli Holten."

Radiance pulsed from her heart-shaped face, and she brushed at long, fat, sausage curls, her hair done in a type popular twenty years earlier. Her smile revealed a slight gap between her upper front teeth. The overall effect had Eli Holten instantly reduced to a love-sick schoolboy. He wanted to whoop and holler, but merely dropped as though stunned into the chair held by a colored waiter.

"Another bourbon, suh?" the waiter asked softly.

Eli found himself quite drunk enough in the presence of such loveliness. "Uh, no thanks. A Lithia water with a lemon slice, please."

"I admire a man of abstinence," Cynthia Gregory declared. "Not a teetotaler, mind. But a man who does not over indulge. Are you bound for the northern frontier on business, Mr. Holten?"

"Please, Eli." Holten frowned slightly, deciding how to explain his mission. "In sort of a way of speaking. I have a friend who has been seriously injured. I'm on the way to see him."

"He must be quite important to you."

"He is, Miss Cynthia. I've known him most of my adult life. He's more like a father to me than just a friend."

"Who might he be?"

"Frank Corrington." Civilian opinion of the military, never high, had reached a new low recently, and he hesitated to be more specific, concerned as he was with making a good impression. What the hell, it would come out sooner or later, he decided. She would or wouldn't think the less of him for being candid. "General Frank Corrington, commanding Fort Rawlins."

Cynthia's cerulean eyes went wide, and her full, sensuous lips puckered into an "Oh." The fingers of one hand fluttered in front of the lace that graced her bodice.

"Oh! Oh, my, I absolutely adore military men." Cynthia's voice grew rapturous. "The dashing, handsome young men, the uniforms, the stirring roll of drums and peal of trumpet, the pagentry and tradition, so romantic."

73

Her description fit little or nothing in Holten's experience. For the sake of conversation, and future plans that formed rapidly in his mind, he would accept her view as accurate.

"Are you a military man, too?" Cynthia asked.

With a start, Eli realized he had been asked a question. "Me? No, I was formerly chief of scouts to General Corrington. I'm now with Crook on the border in Arizona Territory."

Once more his words put Cynthia into flights of romantic fancy. "'Keen-eyed and brave, with intimate knowledge of every path and trail.' I've read my John C. Freemont," she stated proudly.

Surprisingly embarrassed, Holten answered with lowered eyes. "So I see. Freemont tended to wax ro—er, overly enthusiastic in most of his observations."

Cynthia's next words brought Eli's steely gray eyes up to gaze directly into hers. "What's wrong with being romantic?" she asked.

Hot damn! Throughout their meal, somehow Holten managed to respond and carry on a seemingly casual conversation, in which he learned that Cynthia traveled alone for an unspecified purpose, that her father had died gloriously for the Cause—that being, of course, the Confederacy—and that her family was "in cotton" in Natchez, Mississippi. After dinner, they strolled on the promenade deck outside the upper deck public rooms.

Leaning against the stern rail, their hands touched casually. At first contact, Cynthia recoiled chastely, then reached with sudden compulsion and tightly gripped his large fingers. Eli took her into his arms and they kissed. Soft as rose petals, tremulous as a captured bird, her lips fluttered against his, then adhered tightly. Holten grew conscious of her small, firm breasts pressed solidly against his chest. Her scent mingled spring garden with healthy young female.

Well on the way to arousal, Holten pulled her more

74

firmly against him. Her left leg moved, as if to gain better balance, then commenced to rub up and down the outside of his thigh. Eli's kiss grew demanding. Cynthia responded by opening her mouth and slathering his tongue with hers. When their embrace ended, Holten found them both breathless.

"I—ah . . ."

Two small, warm fingers pressed against Eli's lips. "Don't say it. Good soldiers never apologize. Besides," Cynthia added with a hint of a giggle, "I enjoyed it tremendously."

They kissed again, then a third time. Desire became raw and naked in both of their faces. Cynthia squirmed against him and shivered in delight at the pressure of his erect phallus. Holten clasped her buttocks with one big hand and drove her tighter against his rigid member. They both knew in which direction their intimacy led them. When it became obvious that nothing remained to be done, other than consumating their newfound relationship in a bed, Cynthia ended it skillfully.

"I, ah, am sharing my compartment like most everyone. It will take some time to, ah, arrange a reasonable explanation for a prolonged absence. I shall undertake that at once. Then we will have tomorrow night, and many nights after that."

Cynthia rose on tiptoes and kissed him lightly on the lips. Then she was gone.

Holten and Cynthia had breakfast together. Afterward, while Cynthia worked on her cabinmate, Holten sat in on a few hands of poker. He found his fellow players to be poor to average in skill. Slowly the modest stake with which he began started to increase. When he won his fourth pot in a row, a portly man with a completely bald dome tapped stubby fingers on his vest and glowered in the scout's direction.

"You've had remarkable luck for so young a man." A tightly squeezed, petulent voice oozed out of him.

Holten forced a smile. "I'm hardly as young as you might think," he offered affably. "But then, the young are always credited with a willingness to take risks that more experienced men would avoid."

"You sayin' I ain't got guts enough to play poker?" The petulence had grown a fringe of indignation.

"No, not at all. I meant what I said. I even find myself passing up a high-risk draw or folding on the second card where a couple of years ago I would have tried to bludgeon the odds into favoring me."

"A lot of words," the fat man dismissed. "It still seems remarkable that out of the last seven hands, you've won four in a row."

Eli sighed heavily. He could no longer attempt to side-step the implied accusation. He produced a prodigious shrug, which let his right hand slip from the green baize table. Letting ice tinge his words, Holten confronted the hostility between them.

"Are you accusing me of cheating?"

Thick, food-coveting lips pursed into a malignant rosebud. "Every dog knows the stink of its own dung," the offensive poor loser said primly.

Holten's eyes narrowed. "Perhaps you'd like a look up my sleeve? There's an easy way to do that."

His last word hardly uttered, Eli Holten snapped a hard, looping left at the side of the fat man's jaw. His fist connected with a loud, solid smack that toppled his accuser sideways off his chair. It also drew back Eli's coat nearly to the elbow, exposing only a blameless sleeve. Holten gathered his winnings and rose, pocketing them.

"I'll give you gentlemen an opportunity to recover some of this at a more congenial time," he informed the shocked and surprised players.

Holten turned away and started for the door to the salon. On the floor, the fat man darted pudgy fingers into a vest pocket and came out with a shiny flash of nickle plating on a Remington .41 rimfire derringer. The gravel voice of one poker player arrested Holten's movement.

"Look out, mister!"

Instead of turning counter-clockwise, as one ordinarily would, Eli Holten dipped his right shoulder and swung in that direction. His Remington came clear of leather and snapped into line with the back-shooter's face. Absolute silence gripped the salon, except for the loud ratcheting of the hammer notches across the sear.

"Jeeeez," the fat man wheezed through blubbery lips, his porcine jowels quivering.

"Use it or stuff it up your ass. I don't care which," Holten growled.

A ripple started in the crowd near the door, which formed a part so that a short man in a gold-trimmed, blue uniform could pass through. He approached the tense scene with a deliberate stride, face set in an expression of affronted authority.

"Sir," he snapped at Eli Holten's back. "If you please, sir. Lower your firearm. You, too, Mr. Miller," he directed to the man on the floor.

One of the other players reached down and plucked the derringer from Miller's fear-numbed fingers. The uniformed man gave a satisfactory nod as Eli holstered his revolver.

"I'm Captain Andy Hardesty. I believe an explanation is in order."

"Captain, I demand you throw this man off the boat at the next stop. Have him put in irons by the local constable. He's a cardsharp and a cheat."

"Well now, I'm not certain that's a proper request, Mr. Miller."

"Perhaps you didn't listen closely enough, Captain. I didn't 'request,' I demanded it. You are aware of the importance of my position with the company that owns this decrepit tub—"

"I know you got your tit in a wringer with them and are bein' sent out in the sticks to a dead-end job, Mr. Miller." Vern Miller's mouth clapped shut like a snapping turtle while the captain turned to Eli Holten. "Now, sir, you look familiar to me, someone I've had cause to file in memory. A frequent traveler, are you?"

"No. My last trip by steam packet was a bit hectic. I was on the *Natchez Queen* when the boiler blew up."

Captain Andy brightened. "Y-you're that army scout feller, right? The one who saved all those passengers' lives when the *Queen* scattered her hull all over the place. Levi—no—Eli Holten, isn't it?"

"I fear you've found me out," Eli admitted with a chuckle.

"Still working for the army? Haven't taken up gambling for a profession?"

"Yes—and no."

"Well, sir, you're quite a hero to the company." The banty rooster of a captain rocked on his heels and looked up admiringly at Eli Holten. "The president himself put down a letter stating that you are to be our guest whenever you use the river route. Everything is to be made available to you, sir. When we've completed this unpleasant obligation, bring your ticket and your expenses so far to my cabin, behind the pilot house, and I'll reimburse you for monies spent unnecessarily."

"Now see here, Captain. I have given you a specific order, which you will oblige me by obeying," Vern Miller bleated, an edge of nastiness in his tone.

"Ah, yes, something about throwing someone off the *American Eagle*. That I shall most certainly do. And it will be you who is unceremoniously booted onto the dock."

Crimson-faced, his puffy features more piglike than before, Vern Miller ignored the frothy puffs of spittle that formed at the corners of his mouth. "You wouldn't dare. Do as you are told, my good man, if you value your job."

"Oh, I value my job, but I do dare, Mr. Miller. I shall also see that a complete report of your reprehensible behavior is forwarded to the company president."

Quaking in impotent rage, Miller shook a fist at the captain. "You'll rue this day."

Captain Andy crooked his mouth in a fleeting smile and shook his head in denial. "I've long since outlived the time when I cringed from the wrath of self-important nincompoops like you. *I* am the captain of this vessel, and it is I who give the orders aboard her. I suggest you spend your time in a more beneficial manner. Say, packing your belongings. We'll be stopping at around two this afternoon."

"Bu-but that's a w-w-wood station. You said on a dock. You c-ca-can't leave me there."

"Can and will, I'll not have my passengers harassed and insulted by a jackass like you for any longer than necessary. For all I care, you can walk to Wagner. Now, Mr. Hol—ah, Eli, if you will come with me."

"Tell me again how it all happened," Cynthia Gregory coaxed as she lay propped up on one elbow in the double-wide bunk of Eli Holten's cabin.

"You heard it at supper," Holten protested, facing her, his naked body covered by a light sheet.

"Yes, I couldn't help but be curious why the waiters and all made such a fuss over you."

"I also told you all about it on the after promenade." Eli reached out and tweeked a rosebud aureola and small nub of nipple.

"And I want to hear it once more. I want to laugh and enjoy the confounding of the pompous."

"And I, lady, want to explore again in that lush saffron jungle at the juncture of your legs."

Cynthia pinched the loose skin over the hard muscles of Eli's belly. "You're vulgar and uncooth."

79

"Hey, that smarts." Eli affected a pout. "I'll have you know I'm as cooth as the next guy."

Cynthia chuckled deep in her throat, a sensuous, come-hither sound. "I'm not interested in the next guy. Here's the guy who fascinates me." She reached out and wrapped her hand around the flacid bulk of Eli's indominable organ. "He also hurts me like nothing else has ever done."

Eli frowned. "Really? I didn't intend to harm you."

"I know. And it didn't. Just hurt, as in stretched me to the limit, which I dearly love. Truly, nothing has ever done both so perfectly—hurt and pleased."

"Oh? Not even the first time?"

Cynthia's nose crinkled, and her eyes laughed along with her mouth. "Oh, my heavens. I've not thought of that for a long time. My *first* time? I was so excited—scared and incredibly horny—that I hardly felt anything. Besides, it was all such amateurish pushy-push and shovey-shove fumbling out in my oversized playhouse in our backyard, the one I had outgrown, along with dolls, two years before."

"My, only two years after you outgrew dolls and you are flinging away your innocence?" Eli teased.

"Darned right," Cynthia came back heatedly. "I was a woman by nature and past the age of consent, if only thirteen. He was barely two years older than me, but it had taken me a year and a half to get through his thick skull what I'd been after. Then it turned out he didn't know any more about it than me. It was such an embarrassment—all that tussel for little of nothing."

"And now? Do you have that problem now?"

Eyes wide, Cynthia added another hand to his fully risen staff and began to stroke vigorously. "Oh, no. Not in the least, I've truly found the answer to a maiden's prayer."

Eli's strong hands reached out and circled her narrow waist. "Let's see if we can find another answer, or a new prayer." He lifted her free of the bed and swung her

80

slight, graceful form over the top of his massive erection. Slowly he lowered her, her legs spread wide, bent backward at the knee.

She used both hands, one to guide him, the other to spread the pink lips of her well-furred mound. The first contact was blunt and tight, barely encompassing the swollen tip of his curved, swaying cobra. Cynthia made soft, murmuring sounds, and the wiley serpent struck upward, impaling her with a couple of inches.

Inside, the furnace burned hotly. Soft and flowingly wet, yielding with elastic resistance, Cynthia's channel of wonders welcomed him ever so slowly. Arms not yet showing strain, Eli lowered her a bit more. Cynthia squealed with delight. She began to rock and sway in ever-widening circles. ingesting more of his throbbing organ. Fat, blue, pulsing veins slid tantalizingly over her most sensitive parts. Cynthia shivered and begged for more.

Holten raised his knees, and she leaned against them for support, readying herself for the final thrust. "Steady . . . steady . . . NOW!" Eli chanted as he worked her into a frenzy before plunging to the hilt.

Cynthia squealed. She moaned and grunted and gyrated against the fat shaft that had driven to her core. She could feel his rapturous response, gauge the degree of his own frantic arousal. Nothing mattered, nothing else in the world except this time and this place and this blissful joining.

"Now—now . . . ooooh, Eliiiiii!"

Before his own final minute of oblivion, Eli had a crystal jolt of stunning thought. Great as he felt right at that moment, he would go on feeling wonderously euphoric all . . . night . . . long.

CHAPTER 8

Beyond the dust-fogged windows of the Spartan office, horses plodded along the muddy main street of Pierre, Dakota Territory. Children's shrill voices celebrated the last few days before the forced confinement of their six months—May through October—of schooling. Severe weather, with ten and twelve feet of snow on the level and sub-zero temperatures, prevented holding classes during the usual term. A scalded scream of steam whistle on the river announced the departure of the south-bound packet. Bald pate shining in the early morning sunlight, Amos Wade sat at the head of a rectangular oak table. His partners in the Black Hills' exploitation sat opposite each other on the long sides. Amos Wade developed a thunderous scowl as Hez Manning spoke.

"We had lot bigger losses than we should have. Al Handy's worried about keeping the men together."

"Offer them more money," Zach Walters suggested lightly.

"It ain't that, Zack," Manning countered, his thick, blocky, whiskey-barrel body canted forward in agitation. "There's some deserters among them, soldiers who ran from the army to keep from being killed by Injuns. Money won't change their minds, now that they're not in uniform."

Amos Wade had heard enough of the negative side. "Spoken like a true whiskey peddler," he sneered. "You might know Indians, but you've a way to go, Hez, to understand white men. You talk like a man who wants to give up. What happened? Did Holten cut off your balls when he nabbed you for selling rotgut to the Sioux?"

"That sonofabitch! I want Eli Holten dead even more than Frank Corrington," Manning snarled.

"Then we have Al tell the men they'll get a bonus of fifty dollars for every Indian they kill," Wade announced flatly, ignoring Manning's tirade.

"That's a lot of money," Zack Walters said cautiously. "Another raid like that last one and we'd be broke."

Wade snorted derisively. "There'll be another raid, all right. This time against the Sioux. Before it's done, though, there's a little mining camp, Pine Knob. Lots of money there, enough for Handy to be able to pay bonus money for dead Sioux. That's where they're to hit next."

Well north into Nebraska the next morning, excitement rippled through the passengers aboard the *American Eagle*. Their exclamations drew Eli Holten out on deck, his hair still unruly and tossed by Cynthia's passion. He rubbed grit from his eyes and focused on the object of the wild speculation.

Hard-faced and silent, heavily armed, their bodies and horses painted and feather-bedecked, a long file of what appeared to be Sioux and Cheyenne warriors watched the riverboat noisily splash past. Comment died out among the passengers as the steam packet pulled safely away unharmed. A short distance farther along, Eli Holten spotted a cluster of a dozen or so braves grimly watching the progress of the boat. He had little doubt that there would be more.

83

Which set him to considering his reason for being on this boat. Frank Corrington was a tough old bird. He would live or die without the necessity of Eli Holten's presence. Nearing his sixties, Corrington had already lived longer than many men in civilian life. No, it was the *how* of the general's present condition that had spurred Eli into responding instantly.

If Corrington had been ambushed and beaten by Indians, and the sudden appearance of war-painted braves, many reservation jumpers, tended to indicate that, then the army could, and would, solve the problem. Had it been white men, that opened a lot more possibilities. Only the general could say for sure, and he remained lost to the world around him. Either way, the army could make good use of Holten's knowledge of the countryside and its inhabitants. And if Frank died . . . if so, Holten wanted to be on hand when those responsible were captured.

Afternoon found him simularly distracted. He lost thirty dollars at poker before he admitted to himself that he had not been paying attention. Eli cashed in his chips and retired to the stern promenade to smoke a cigar. He would dine with Cynthia Gregory, and then another wonderful night in bed with her. Eli found that sufficient to wrest his mind from anticipation of what waited for him at Fort Rawlins. Meanwhile his occupation had become known to fellow passengers, Eli noted when a well-dressed, nervously fussy man with a bowler and cane approached him.

"Pardon me, I understand you work for the army, a scout is it?" The prim mouth under gold-rim spectacles worked with enough agitation to cause a pencil-line of mustache above it to wriggle wormlike.

"Uh—yes, I am."

A short exhalation of relief. "I was wondering . . . those, ah, those savages we saw this morning? Were they hostiles?"

"Without any arrows or bullet holes in the smokestacks, I'd say no. You understand, that doesn't mean they were friendly. Only that they weren't making war on us."

The man in the bowler swallowed hard. "What tribe were they?"

"Cheyenne for the most part. Ordinarily they don't come this far east. Some Sioux, who should be on the reservation. Later I saw a group of Pani," Holten added, using the Lakota word for the Pawnee.

"Is there something unusual about that?"

Holten shrugged. Might as well frighten the britches off this dude as leave him wringing his hands for nothing. "To get them, or the Omaha, to wearing paint takes some doing. You can be certain there's some kind of trouble northwest of us."

"In the direction we're heading?" The little man actually paled.

"My guess is beyond the Black Hills, Montana or Wyoming. But the word gets around among the tribes, and unrest comes with it."

Holten's interrogator sighed and asked hopefully, "Then, they are just showing their disapproval? Sort of flexing their muscles?"

"Something like that," Holten assured him. "Though I wouldn't jump off this boat and try to discuss it with them."

"I—ah—see. Well, er, thank you, Mr. Holten."

Holten watched him walk away and snorted in disgust. Damned if the dude hadn't gotten him back to thinking about the implications of armed and painted warriors watching the river.

Eli Holten sat naked on the edge of the bunk, all scarred and hairy. His long, fat penis curved rigidly upward from a thick thatch of damp, light brown hair at its base. Cynthia Gregory knelt on a pillow between his legs. She made soft, rhythmic slurping sounds as

85

she bobbed her head up and down in an attempt to take more of his manhood deep into the silken moistness of her mouth. Sighing, Holten leaned backward, supported on his outstretched arms.

"Oooh, Cindy—Cindy, you're a marvel," he gusted out. "More . . . take more of it."

Cynthia obliged with a big gulp. With more than half of his massive machinery encased in her suctioning mouth, Eli began to reflexively thrust his hips. Cynthia made appreciative throat noises and cupped his scrotum with one hand. She kneaded his stones in a delightful manner, sending new storms of erotic sensation through Eli's body. Her tongue, darting about the exposed bulb, gave further pleasure. Eli's belly tightened, and his senses reeled.

Infinitesimally short of climactic explosion, Cynthia withdrew from the object of her affection and clambered onto the bed. "Take me, Eli," she moaned. "Take me like a raging stallion."

She positioned herself on hands and knees, legs wide-spread, and looked beseechingly at him over one shoulder. Aching from the build-up of unrelieved sap, Eli came to his feet and approached her, huge phallus swaying with his movement. Carefully he slid his red, wet member between her buttocks and along the short path to her poised cleft. He pierced the pouting lips and plunged through leafy portals with enough force to seat him deeply. Cynthia squealed and wriggled her posterior.

Eli cleaved her like a wedge. sinking to the hilt. Then he began to piston his hips. Mewing cries came from Cynthia's strained lips, matched by the grunts of effort the scout made to excite them both. Carefully he gauged himself, prolonging the ultimate, drawing more and more from the well that he so vigorously plumbed.

"Aayyyyyeeee-liiiiii!" Cynthia wailed as a magnificent climax shook her to the core.

"Stay with me . . . stay with me," Eli urged, thundering toward his own magnificent dissolution.

From far off they heard music, muted strings and a chorus of ecstatic voices. Eli grabbed handholds on her flared hips and churned along in utter fascination. Her inner workings gripped at him and retarded the long, shivering retreats, and sprang wide to receive the powerful upward lunges. Time became endurance, and the race went to Eros as they surrendered to euphoric oblivion together.

"Oh, my—my—my, I'll never—never forget you, Eli Holten," Cynthia crooned several minutes later as they lay side by side and sipped champagne from crystal flute glasses.

"I'm sure I got more than I gave," Eli murmured.

"Not possible," Cynthia protested. "I thought that beast of yours would kill me. Happily it didn't, so I could enjoy it more and more. Had it done so, I would have died a contented woman."

Holten's hand found one breast and cupped it, thumb and forefinger teasing the nipple. A jolt of fine delight shot through him as Cynthia closed her hand around his semi-erect organ. She manipulated it with expert skill, and Eli thought of the erotic confidences they had shared together the night before. Arousal came with review.

"Oh, Eli, I think you're ready for more."

"I know I am, Cindy," Eli breathed close to her ear.

With all the eager energy of a horny teen, Eli rolled onto her supine form, one hand spreading her legs, seeking out the damp mound so recently assaulted from behind. He found it dripping and ready. Cynthia gave his great shaft an affectionate squeeze and directed it to the lips of Venus. There he took over and began to tease her to higher excitement by sliding the bulb tip up and back, barely inside the outer portal.

Cynthia squealed and uttered short "aaah-unnh-aaaahs." Then, when she believed she would burst asunder with desire, he took her swiftly, hilting himself in a single, long drive. Her head filled with stars. Holten's long, lean body swayed above her as he used his arms to support himself while his pistoning hips drove his rigid maleness into her sweet confines. Cynthia raised her legs and entwined them around his waist.

Then, with a terrible crash, the cabin door burst open and slammed back against the outer wall. "You goddamned homewrecker!" a young man screamed in almost a soprano register. "I've caught you and this vile seducer together at last."

The slender intruder stood in the doorway, a seven shot .32 revolver dangling from one hand. His eyes wild, they darted an unsteady glance around the room, centering on the bunk. Slowly he raised the revolver.

"Get out of here, Randy," Cynthia groaned, covering her nakedness with a sheet."

Eli Holten had sprung apart from her at the first tearing sound of the broken latch. He landed on the floor in the far corner of the room, his .44 Remington revolver in hand and ready. "Who the hell are you?" he growled, body aching from interrupted fulfillment.

"I'm her husband, you dastardly knave!" the small, slender young man tremoloed.

Did he actually say 'dastardly knave'? Holten couldn't believe what he heard.

"No, he's not!" Cynthia shrieked. "Not any more."

Any more? Eli swallowed hard. "You've broken into my cabin, mister. You'd better have your ass out the door in two seconds or I'll put some holes through you."

"Cuckhold I am, but I shall be avenged." The patois of Mississippi thickened his speech.

Eli Holten wanted to laugh. The dialogue so far sounded like a poorly done melodrama, or an amateurish attempt at the old badger game. Either way, it had grown stale, and the Maynard revolver was only too real.

"I like to know the name of a man before I kill him," Holten growled for effect.

Their unwanted visitor blinked. "It's Randolph Simpson," Cynthia Gregory's voice came from under the sheet. "Oh, Randy, why do you have to be such a—such an ass?" she asked miserably.

Lower lip trembling, Simpson made his answer to her. "You betrayed me Cindy. But I can forgive you. You've been blinded by this—this depraved purveyor of innocent flesh. Come, my beloved, let me take you away from all this."

While Randy unreeled his pompous declaration, Eli Holten came to his feet. In two swift strides he reached the young intruder's side and snatched the weapon from Randy's grasp. Eli's other hand held the light-weight fellow by the scruff of the neck. Unarmed and helpless, Randy's rage remained.

"Unhand my wife, sir. She's coming with me."

"Seems to me it's you I'm holding on to," Holten observed.

"I'm not your wife!" Cynthia wailed.

"See? See? He's addled your mind. . . ." Randy raged on.

"I left you a year ago, you sorry little man," Cynthia responded, her voice on the edge of humility.

"B-but we're married," Randy stammered.

"No we're not. A marriage has to be *consumated* before it's valid. What that means, my dear ex-husband, is that you have to get it up, and keep it up, long enough to get it in."

Suddenly deflated, Randy Simpson shrank in Eli Holten's grasp. "Don't be vulgar, Cynthia. Now, sir, if you'll release me?" Holten did so, and Simpson reached into a vest pocket. He produced a calling card, which he extended to Eli. "You have sullied my wife's fair name and distorted her mind. I demand satisfaction."

"Satis—awh, hell, kid," Eli responded disgustedly. "When do you ask for the money?"

"What money?" Randolph Simpson blinked owl-ishly, totally confused.

"The shake-down money. What else is the badger game for?" Eli grumbled.

"Wha-what's a badger game?" Randolph gulped.

"Oh, never mind, just get the hell out of here."

"No. Not until you agree to give me satisfaction."

"I'll give you a kick in the as—" Holten snarled.

"What's all this ruckus?" Captain Andy interrupted to ask.

"Oh, ah, Captain," Eli gulped. "I was entertaining, and—"

"Ah, yes. I can see," Captain Andy broke in, grinning, his twinkling eyes taking in Eli's nakedness and the obviously female figure under the sheet. "You want this feller removed, Mr. Holten?"

"It would help, Captain. Where did he come from?"

"Got aboard the last stop. And he'll be going off at the next one. Come along, sonny."

"Captain, I demand, I insist . . . I . . ." Randolph Simpson railed as Captain Andy marched him out of the cabin.

With order restored, the door closed and barred in place with a straight-back chair, and his sixgun in its holster, Eli Holten turned to make a final inspection of the small cubicle. "Stop fussing, Eli, and come over here," Cynthia coaxed in a throaty voice.

"Ummm. I'll do that, but after our little visitor, I'm fairly sure all we can do is sleep. Like poor Randy, I don't think I can get it up."

Eli slid beneath the sheet, and Cynthia's hands rushed to his groin. "Oh . . . yes . . . you . . . can!" she chortled gleefully a few minutes later.

CHAPTER 9

Bansheelike, the steam whistle of the *American Eagle* screeched as the packet neared the bend. Riding the spring thaw, the banks were not so high as to block out sight of any on-coming traffic, but Captain Andy believed in following the rules of the road. When approaching a bend in the river, a steamboat always sounded its whistle. Body still humming with the salutary effects of a long night of energetic loving, Eli Holten studied the passing terrain, noting landmarks that told him of passing the invisible boundary between Nebraska and Dakota Territory. Isolated by space and time from the Apache campaign behind him and the unknown troubles ahead, he basked in a blessed calm.

Eli had dismissed the whole incident of the night before. There had been no suggestion of a payoff, so he felt certain that Cindy's explanation was correct. He was equally positive that no possibility existed for the bumbling Mississippian, Simpson, carrying out his demand for a duel. That settled and dismissed, he went in to breakfast.

Coffee smelled heart-achingly delicious. A big, polished silver urn steamed against the forward wall of the dining room. Eli stopped there first, before giving any thought at all to the buffet arranged down one long side. His first sip told him the beans had come from

New Orleans, fresh-ground that morning. His second confirmed that they had certainly not had this blend on previous mornings. Laced with too-thick-to-pour spoon cream, it became ambrosia. By the time he finished the first cup, his stomach growled for an introduction to food.

Heated by a line directly from the boilers, the steam table contained an insert of three types of sausage, another of ham and side pork strips, with a third of fried, pan-sized, whole catfish. Another tray held a mound of fluffy, yellow scrambled eggs, and a third contained potatoes, with a smaller insert of grits at the side. There was also apple sauce and fruit perserves to put on fresh biscuits, cornbread and flap jacks. Eli Holten broke custom and ate like a starved field hand.

Keeping up with Cynthia demanded it. She appeared when he had worked halfway through his first plate. She selected some ham, a sparing daub of grits and a single biscuit. She came directly to his table. Eli gave her a big, hearty good morning and a smile of equal size. Cynthia responded demurely and took the seat he held for her.

"There'll be a stop in an hour," she remarked after their greetings.

"I know. A wood camp. Don't worry, Captain Andy won't maroon your ex-husband there."

"I wouldn't care if he did. What concerns me is that Randy may try to make good on his demand for satisfaction. He's very . . . Southern."

Holten laughed lightly. "Don't be upset by it. Chances are he won't show his face outside the captain's cabin, or wherever Captain Andy stuck him away last night."

Holten's uncanny ability to often predict events failed him. No sooner had the *American Eagle* tied up to take on a load of cordwood for the boiler fires than Randolph Vickers Simpson came bounding down the springy gangplank and hustled over to Captain

Andy and the chief engineer. He had a long, cherry-wood box tucked under his left arm.

"Come along now, Captain, be a good sport. I need you to function as a judge. You, too, Engineer Greer. And I . . . I suppose the pilot can act as Holten's second. Mr. Phillips, a first-class passenger, has agreed to assist me. You, Captain, see that Mr. Holten is prepared and offer him choice of weapons." He offered the handsome case.

Inside Captain Andy found an exquisite matched pair of dueling pistols.

"After Holten has made his choice, you and Mr. Greer can load them."

When Eli heard what Simpson had in store, he laughed good-naturedly. "I'm not going to duel with him. Hell, the sprout wouldn't have a chance."

"He's serious," Captain Andy informed his honored guest. "Wouldn't do for him to go bandying about that you were a coward, now would it?"

Eli looked askance at the captain. "Are you promoting this duel?"

"Horsefeathers! Of course not, Eli. Only . . ." He ended with an elaborate shrug.

"He might take it in mind to back-shoot me," Eli concluded wearily.

"He is a most determined young man."

Again Eli cocked his head and eyed the skipper. "Come on, now. Oh, hell, all right. He isn't going to do something stupid like demanding this be to the death, is he?"

"I'll tell him he'll be held for murder if he does," Captain Andy said with a wink.

"Then we'll go through with it. It's a damned farce, but what can I do?" Eli asked rhetorically.

Randolph Simpson fairly beamed with excitement when the boat's officers returned to inform him that Eli Holten had made his choice. He then supervised the loading and nodded in satisfaction. With a dramatic, full-arm gesture, he indicated a flat stretch of clear ground where ricks of wood were normally stored.

"That will serve nicely. Mr. Phillips, if you please?"

Ten minutes later Captain Andy and Mr. Greer had everything arranged. Following a dusty memory of the ritual, Captain Andy asked the aggrieved party if there could be any chance for reconciliation.

"Definitely not," Simpson snapped.

"Then we will begin. Gentlemen, stand here, please, back to back. This affair of honor will be fought with first blood for honor satisfied."

"I have every intention of killing this defiler of fair womanhood," Simpson said icily.

"You do and I'll see you hanged for murder," Captain Andy growled.

"It will be worth it."

Captain Andy cast a desperate look at Eli Holten. Eli merely nodded. "Very well. When I say, 'begin,' you will commence to take ten paces apart, at the count. When I say, 'halt,' you will stop. I will then say, 'turn.' At which point each of you turns to face the other. At my command, 'on guard,' you will aim your pistols. When I give the order, 'fire,' you will discharge your pistols. Good luck to both of you, and may the better man win."

"Victory is on the side of right," Simpson uttered tight-lipped.

"Ready?" the nervous river pilot asked Eli Holten. The scout gave a curt nod. "You may begin."

"Begin," Captain Andy Hardesty droned. "One—two—three—four—five . . ." The count continued while excited passengers enjoyed vicarious participation. "HALT!"

"One last appeal in the name of humanity, gentlemen," Holten urged. "Will you lay this quarrel aside?"

"Never!" Simpson shouted.

"Ah—well. Turn. On guard. May God defend the right." He didn't know if it belonged there, but it sounded good. "Fire."

Randolph Simpson's dueling pistol discharged a fraction of a second before Eli Holten's. The ball kicked up dust between Eli's legs. Then the hammer fell on the ornate, silver chased pistol in Eli's hand, and flame from the cap ignited the powder. A grunt and soft cry came from Randolph Simpson, and he clapped his left hand over the top of his right shoulder.

At once the seconds, judges and official witnesses rushed to Simpson's side. Blood streamed between his fingers. "Blood has been drawn," Captain Andy announced.

"Honor has been satisfied," Mr. Greer declared. "Gentlemen shake hands and dismiss this from your memory."

"Not likely," Simpson snarled.

"Civilization," Eli Holten grumbled.

Somewhere, on the far side of the village, women still mourned the dead. White Horse came to Shutai, forehead ridged with deep gullies. His chest ached and felt swollen with the anger and grief that filled him. Shutai, a competent and kindly civil chief, had tested the climate of the people before this meeting. He knew what they all wanted.

He also knew that it would result in tragedy and defeat. Half of their people had been forcibly removed south to the white man's Indian Territory. The rest would be sent that way, too, if they participated in a general uprising. Shutai didn't want that. He also didn't want the whites to go unpunished for violating the treaty and murdering the women and children at the Little River camp.

"I have come to talk of war," White Horse began without preamble.

"I would speak of peace," Shutai responded.

White Horse studied the old man's wrinkles. They

95

radiated from around eyes accustomed to squinting in harsh sunlight for more than fifty summers. Shutai's high, seamed forehead spoke of the wisdom accumulated behind it. White Horse had always respected the venerated civil chief. While still a boy he had followed the then powerful warrior around, mimicking exactly his arrogant strut. And he, too, had believed when Shutai spoke of peace with the white man. No more. His own village had been wiped out. His wife and one child killed. Thirty men survived to mourn for wives, children, fathers, mothers. Thirty warriors who demanded justice.

"I will take up the war pipe and see who will follow me," White Horse stated flatly.

Shutai noted the lack of challenge, the words of White Horse a statement of fact, not a boast or dare. Nor had it been a request, as was proper. He sighed heavily, and his gnarled left hand strayed to the fringed and beaded elk-hide case of the war pipe. "You do so without my blessing."

Eyes narrowing, White Horse made an abbreviated move toward the pipe. "You would see us all killed?"

"No, my son . . . you would. But that's not the consideration here, is it? The mark of a good leader is to see that the people are protected, and that they get what they want. So take the pipe of war and carry it proudly; many will follow you. Only know that I do not wish it so, though no man can turn back the rising waters. Count coup on some for me, White Horse."

Elated, yet careful to maintain a straight face, White Horse bent low to grasp the pipe. "I will, Grandfather."

Within a day's ride, White Horse made good his promise. Forty-five warriors rode past the settlement of Belle Fourche and attacked a homestead ranch to the southeast. They burned the buildings, and their coup sticks touched the three men, two women and five children who lived there. No one died in that place. The vengeful Cheyenne came upon the mining camp of Burnt Water before dawn the next day.

It had been men dressed like these who had attacked his camp, White Horse recalled when he looked down a long slope to the cluster of shacks, tents and sluiceways. Their greed for the yellow metal kept the place ablaze with light in the dark time so that they could work through the night. Such men could not be normal. White Horse deployed his force and waited for the opportune moment.

That came when a piercing clang erupted from a bent metal rod that hung outside the largest structure in the camp. The white men laid aside their tools and started for the building from which cooking food odors had assailed the Cheyenne for a finger's width of time. White Horse produced a grim smile and raised his repeating rifle in his broad, strong hand to give the signal to attack.

"WHOO-keeee-yiiiii-yiiiii-whooo!"

Echoing off the hillsides, the haunting war cry shocked men to immobility inside the dining hall. Several froze with forks of biscuit and gravy partway to their mouths. Others made jerky motions to rise, only to arrest all movement. Another chilling whoop split the morning. Hoofbeats thudded on the pine needle ground cover. A rifle cracked and, a man screamed out by the sluicebox.

Released as one from their stasis, the men ran around the dining hall in mindless confusion. Two miners, near the front door. yanked sixguns from their holsters and rushed outside. Pincushioned by arrows, one staggered back inside, to gasp and fall dead.

"Oh, Christ, it's the Cheyenne," one burly miner blurted.

"I tol' ya, Red, I tol' ya. We shouldn't have gone with those fellers to that village. They're gonna kill us all," another babbled.

Bullets broke windows as the Cheyenne rode in

97

among the few exposed miners. Rifles cracked on both sides, and bowstrings twanged. In seconds the vulnerable whites had all fallen within a few feet of where they had been when the attack began. By that time a number of the more level-headed inside the cook shack had armed themselves and left the building by the back door. They ran to positions that offered at least partial cover and opened fire on the attacking force.

Directed by two of Al Handy's hardcases, they immediately had telling effect. Cool, well-aimed fire knocked three warriors from their ponies and alerted White Horse to this new challenge. At once his compact force broke into smaller groups and individuals. Whirling off to the flanks, they kept up a steady pressure on the defenders.

Here and there a bullet or arrow found flesh and a miner screamed in agony or died, often silently with only a harsh grunt to mark the man's demise. Inexorably the line of white men thinned. White Horse rode to a vantage point where he could look down on the besieged whites.

"Long Nose, Two Spirits," he commanded. "Take men, get around behind them and be ready to ride them down. Wait for my signal."

"We will dance their scalps at tomorrow's night-fires," Long Nose shouted proudly.

White Horse gave other orders, and men rushed to carry them out. When he saw the warriors in position behind the defenders, he gave his signal and rushed with twenty men toward the dining hall. Under cover of this advance, other braves rose up with fire arrows and dispatched their terrible projectiles to the roof and walls of the crowded building.

Flames bit hungrily into the resinous wood. Smoke began to swirl in the light sunrise breeze, obscuring the battlefield. A rattle of rifle fire to his right told White Horse that the surprise had been complete on the white men fighting outside. Again he raised his arm and gave another signal.

Before the threatened defenders could regroup, all the buildings, tents and supply sheds blazed around them. Even the sluicebox and wooden flume burned. Men inside the dining hall discovered the fire and yelled in fright. Singly at first, then in a concerted rush they ran from the doomed structure.

Yelping, hooting Cheyenne warriors cut them down without mercy. When the last arrow flew and the final round cracked from White Horse's repeating rifle, some twenty miners and the trio of Handy hardcases lay dead among the ruins of the camp. White Horse sat his war pony, hard-faced and unforgiving while the wounded were dispatched.

Now the scalping could begin. Little River camp had been revenged.

"Now dammit, Howard, I can't look at a wound and tell you how it happened, or who did it," Major Wallace Jansen complained. "The general is still unconscious. How long he remains like that is still as unknown as the day your troops brought him in here."

"Isn't there anything you can do?" Lieutenant Colonel Mayberry urged.

Jansen shrugged both shoulders in his white surgeon's coat. "Anything I might do has a better chance of hurrying the condition in the direction we don't want it to go. You knew all of this a week ago. Why are you pestering me again?"

"We just got a directive from Headquarters. I for one don't like it one damn bit. Sam's not happy, either. We sent a request for another general officer to take temporary command."

"Don't tell me. They denied your request, right?"

"Umm-hum. Instead, they shuffled us around some and left the bag in our hands. Greg Bellknap is to administer the business of the fort, while Sam has tactical command of the infantry and I have the cavalry."

"Well, that sounds reasonable," Major Jansen offered.

"You can't run an army post with a fucking committee. In particular you can't run a brigade headquarters. But there aren't any spare general officers. At least that's what St. Paul said."

"Meanwhile we have white attacks against Indian villages clear the hell over in Wyoming and hostiles raising a gawd-awful ruckus all over the Black Hills," Colonel Britton groused as he stepped into the hospital room of his comatose commander.

"While the territorial governor sits on his hands and diddles himself," Mayberry took up their litany of woe. "At least Eli Holten should be here any day now. His telegram said he would take the 'swiftest possible means of travel.'"

"What good can he do?" Major Jansen asked doubtfully.

A small hint of a smile quirked the corners of Mayberry's mouth. "He is detached from this command, and also from Crook's. Technically, he is a free agent and can act however he sees fit. At risk of being called a guardhouse lawyer, I think I can confidently say that even a court martial board would see it that way."

Jansen brightened. "It sounds like you two have cooked up something?"

Sam Britton nodded. "That we have. Suppose—just suppose, mind you—that Holten happens to find out something. And suppose he conveys that information to some of Frank's friends among the NCOs, and from them the leading rankers learn about it. Then suppose they all happen to put in for leave at the same time and it's granted. Don't you suppose that it would then make sense for Eli Holten to lead them on a little expedition to kick ass on those responsible for what happened to Frank?"

"But they're still soldiers, under orders to not mix in," the surgeon protested.

"On leave, they're *technically* not subject to that order. The most we would be compelled to do," Howard Mayberry explained, "would be to hold an inquiry, fine them a month's pay and cut orders to transfer them to other commands."

"Well and good, now tell me how that all fits in with the state of hostilities between whites and the red man?" Jansen prodded.

"It's all interrelated, if you want my opinion," Colonel Britton snapped.

"Mine, too," Mayberry supported the brigade executive officer. "One is merely an aspect of the other. Someone wanted Frank out of the way in order to further one scheme or another. We—we just haven't figured out what as yet."

"Meanwhile, and I don't like to be trite, gentlemen, the whole frontier is ready to burst into flame," Jansen added.

"Shit!" Colonel Britton exploded.

Looking sheepish, Lieutenant Colonel Mayberry added, "Which makes this latest flash of wisdom from Department Headquarters gall the more. We have been reminded that the civil authorities know what they are doing and not to involve our troops unless specifically requested by the governor."

"And that won't happen until we're wading asshole-deep in hostiles on the parade ground," Colonel Britton added grimly.

CHAPTER 10

Brown thrashers and redstarts offered final, bright, cheery promises in defiance of the sorrowful dirge of the mourning doves. Doreen Thorne set down the cleanly wiped tin plate and smacked her lips in appreciation of the rich, savory antelope stew prepared by the wranglers of the Belle Fourche Cattle Company. The buckboard and two-wheel cart driven by Doreen and Samantha formed part of the semi-circular laager along with the chuckwagon and supply wagon. Thus backed against a low hill, the night camp had settled safely until a new day. Their horses munched grain for the first time since the journey began, tethered to a picket line along with the draft animals of the cowboys. Doreen exchanged glances with her sisters and nodded in unspoken agreement.

She rose in furtherance of their decision and walked to where a gangling youth of about seventeen stood by the fire. Smiling in her most winsome and willing manner, Doreen put a soft hand on his arm.

"You fellers did right nice by us, Jake. We—ah—we are mightily obliged to you. We—ah, want to make it up to y'all, show our gratitude."

Doreen stepped closer and, masked by their bodies, reached out with her other hand to squeeze the area behind Jake's trouser fly. It left no doubt as to how they

102

would give their thanks. Jake grinned like a boobie. His heart thudded in his chest, and his Adam's apple jerked dramatically up and down when he swallowed hard. Over Doreen's shoulder, he saw little Helen approach Sammy, the skullery boy.

Helen whispered something in the preteen's ear that made him blush and squeal like a pig. She patted the suddenly appearing bulge in his whipcord trousers and took his hand to lead him behind a low screen of ground hemlock. Melissa Thorne chuckled, low and throatily, as she led the foreman toward his soogans. Smanatha and Susanna set their sights on two gangling youths in their late teens. Giggling in anticipation, Samantha, the boldest of the five Thorne girls, called lightly to the remaining astounded cowboys.

"Don't y'all worry. There's enough for everybody. We'll be back in just a little while to take care of ev'ry little thing."

Lulled by the sonorous splash of water over the churning sidewheels of the *American Eagle,* Eli Holten stretched languidly on his bunk beside the eternally exciting, naked form of Cynthia Gregory. They had spent most of their last night on board in a passionate good-bye. So far Eli had learned little of her plans. She knew only that he was headed for Fort Rawlins. Holten stirred and reached for the champagne bottle.

"Tomorrow morning we'll be in Pierre," he remarked. "Where do you go from there?"

Cynthia ran fingernails down the knobs of Eli's spine. "Camp Sturgis on the edge of the Black Hills," she stated with a resigned sigh.

"The army post?" Eli asked, not expecting that answer.

"Yes." Another sigh. "I haven't said anything, dear Eli, because—because I didn't want—well, I didn't want anything to spoil our—this precious, wonderful time we've had together."

Holten frowned and handed her a glass of bubbling wine. "How do you mean that?"

"I . . . well, I'm on my way to Camp Sturgis to be married to an army officer who's stationed there. He's from Fort Reno, where I'll live." With the stopper removed she let the story flow in a torrent of words. "It was all arranged by my father. After I left poor Randy, he felt it best for me to acquire a husband, one more mature and—ah—proficient, and preferably one removed from Mississippi. My—intended is in his late thirties, a mature man, and this is a second marriage for both of us. He has two small children, under ten. His wife died of some strange frontier malady. I—I'm sorry, Eli. I didn't intend to deceive you. I just—for some reason, this—our encounter—seemed to be so necessary for me."

Holten sipped champagne and scowled fleetingly. "Go on."

"What I mean is that this free-spirited interlude of mine came about because I wanted to have a 'real' man before settling down to a dreary reality with two stepchildren, an absentee husband and the squalor of a frontier fort to contend with."

"So you picked me for your real man, eh?" Holten inquired grumpily.

"Oh, Eli, it wasn't like that, so cold, calculating. I didn't say eeny-meeny-miney and pick you. It—just sort of happened, and it was wonderful. Once we got started, I couldn't say no. Or—or tell you everything."

Not at all happy about this arrangement, Holten let himself remain perturbed for a few long, ticking minutes. Then Cynthia giggled and lunged toward him, graceful arms twining around his neck, legs spread wide and clutching at the outside of his thighs. The moist warmth of her mound pressed against his pubic arch and brought immediate response. Stiffening, Eli's well-used member rose to bisect the rosy cleft that sought to surround it.

"Oh, Eli, you're more than just a real man. You're more man than any woman has a right to dream of. I'll always cherish this time we have enjoyed, carry it as a reminder of what the Muslim paradise must be like. Don't be angry with me. Don't chide me for my womanly wiles. I—I really didn't want to hurt you with the truth. B-but I can't deny you anything."

Bemused by her rampant sexuality, innocence mixed with abandon, Eli surrendered himself to the tender demands of the flesh. He would, he vowed silently, make this last night one to remember.

Mason Ashford stood facing the three hard men with an inner trepidation that the power of his angry message from Governor Stratton could not dispell. He had delivered the message in, he believed, a properly stern manner. Instead of quailing in abject contrition before the wrath of the governor as was fitting, this arrogant peasant, Amos Wade, spoke most shockingly.

"I don't give a shit what the governor thinks, sonny-boy," he growled. "He wanted trouble stirred up, and we, by God, got it that way. Now, if he's worth half the hot air that old fart spouts, he'd better come through with his end. It's time to have the militia alerted and made ready to go avenge the massacre of those poor, innocent miners."

"B-but you have completely misunderstood his orders to go easy for a while," Ashford protested with a lisp.

"I have intentionally ignored such an asinine suggestion from someone who seems to have forgotten his place in all this. Stratton—and by implication you, sonny—is a silent partner. Which means that he remains silent. We get the ideas and we give the orders. He earns his share by being accommodating. Now get out of here, we have an important noon luncheon meeting with a railroad representative at the Prentiss House."

Mason Ashford fled from the sparsely furnished office with alacrity. With each step that carried him farther from his humiliation, his mind produced another "What if I'd said . . ." or "I should have punched that fat fool . . ." and even, "Next time, I'll. . . ." They were truly dangerous men, and his fantasies helped keep him from weeping.

Then new terror came to abide in Mason Ashford's timerous breast. What would the governor say? What would he do?

Pierre, Dakota Territory. And the Prentiss House. Until he could find out who and what might be heading for Fort Rawlins, Eli Holten checked into the best hotel in town. A bellboy took his sparse belongings to the room and left the key, in exchange for a tip. A scant half hour before noon, Holten had time on his side. He washed his hands and face, more from habit than necessity, and straightened his clothes. Then he went downstairs to the comfortable, ground-floor saloon.

Standing at the bar, Eli surveyed the occupants of the room. "Do you have a Napoleon brandy?" he inquired.

"Yes, sir. Two as a matter of fact. Remy Martin and Chateau La Rochelle."

"I'll have the Martin, and one of those skinny cigars in the yellow box."

"Right away, sir. Are you a guest of the hotel?"

"Yeah."

"Would you like to sign for this and have it added to your bill?"

Holten shrugged. He'd never encountered that service before. "Sure, why not?"

He'd worked halfway through the first brandy when

three prosperously dressed men, whose fine clothes could not hide the crudeness of their natures, entered together and selected a table. The youngest of the trio hailed the bartender.

"Oscar, we'll have the usual. And has the gentleman from the UP arrived as yet?"

"Coming right up, and no, sir, he has not," the barman answered.

"Have a bellboy check the lobby and dining room. The name's Wainwright."

"Right away, sir."

Holten found himself slouching some, his face in a pool of shadow. He studied the three men closely. Something about them seemed quite familiar. He should know their names. Know more about them than that, some instinct prompted him. By the time he finished his brandy and consumed a second, inspiration had failed to ignite him. He shrugged and departed to put out the word.

Through most of the afternoon, Eli went about town, asking after immigrant or supply trains, mail delivery, army details or any travelers headed southwest to Fort Rawlins. He had no success, though the whole community knew he sought information of such. On his way back to the Prentiss House, he again saw the three men, who strolled along the boardwalk with a proprietary air. He entered the hotel and went directly to the dining room.

Holten had consumed several beers during the course of his search for travel companions. For that reason he declined a drink before eating. He ordered his supper sparingly and sipped at a scalding cup of coffee while waiting for the food to arrive. His thoughts went again to the familiar faces.

Although the years had gone by, Eli's memory finally provided names for the three men. While he finished his evening meal, he worked the names over in his head. Amos Wade. The bald one had to be him. The one with the walk of a gunfighter must be Zacharia Walters, and the youngest could be Hezakiah Manning. They must all have been recently released from prison. He and Frank had sent each of them there, Eli recalled, for crimes committed in the territory.

Manning was a gunrunner and whiskey peddler. Eli had caught him at it and seen him sentenced to ten years hard labor. Walters had murdered a young Sioux couple, the son of a chief and his new bride, and nearly caused a general uprising along the frontier. Eli had hunted him down, and testimony from Frank Corrington had helped put him away. Amos Wade had sold non-existant gold mines to the whites and disease-infected blankets to the Sioux. He had also run a large, prosperous ranch, populated with stolen cattle. Again, Eli and Frank had put Wade behind bars.

Something teased Holten's sixth sense. On the way across the lobby, he thought on it and smiled sardonically at the revelation. He hadn't been in town an hour and he'd come across three men with excellent reasons for hating Frank Corrington and himself. He'd keep that in mind, he decided, although one fact mitigated against any involvement by Wade and his cronies. If they had recognized him, they had given no sign of it.

In his box at the desk, Eli found a note, a response to the feelers he'd put out earlier. "Mr. Holten," it read. "A supply column is making up and will depart for Fort Rawlins tomorrow morning at 0900. You are welcome to travel along. And welcome back. Cpl. Chris Newcomb."

Smiling, Eli Holten retired to his room for the night in an improved mood.

Frogs and crickets vied for dominance in the inky blackness of a moonless night. In a tumble-down, unpainted shack on the edge of Pierre, with the muddy water of the Missouri River lapping at the pilings of a small, weathered dock behind the wretched dwelling, Amos Wade and Hez Manning met with Al Handy.

"Dammit, it's getting too dangerous with Eli Holten back in the territory. If Corrington regains consciousness and tells what he knows. . . ." Hezakiah Manning broke off to let the thought hang heavily in the slovenly room.

"Don't be an old woman, Hez," Amos Wade growled. "So long as Holten can't talk to Corrington, we have nothing to worry about. Perhaps . . ." he paused, painfully conscious of their last failure. "Perhaps what we need to do is make another try on Corrington."

"We did," Al Handy reminded them needlessly. "The army's not letting any civilians into the dispensary at Fort Rawlins. On top of that, from what my men could find, the general's too well guarded for them to have succeeded anyway."

An idea grew for Amos Wade. "Then what we need is to send soldiers after him. Then Holten can be taken care of. Stop the both of them and our way is clear."

"Do you have any idea how long it would take to recruit one soldier, let alone three or four, to commit a murder right in the middle of an army post?" Al Handy protested.

Wade raised a hand in a calming gesture. "Take it easy, Al. We don't have to use *real* soldiers. We can get our hands on plenty of uniforms. Even some white hospital coats. All you need do, Al, is provide bodies to fill them. They'll need to be mighty smart," he cautioned. "Able to think on their feet and adapt to changing circumstances. Surely you have a few like that?"

"Of course I do. I can name you three or four right off hand," Al stated confidently.

"Good. Be ready to put the plan into operation.

Here's what they'll be expected to do. . . ."

Fat and red, a bloated sun hung on the horizon when Eli Holten approached the circle of freight wagons at the western edge of Pierre. A lean, angular, young corporal produced a prodigious yawn and stretched with tomcat pleasure as the scout strolled within the ring. The noncom developed a white smile in his leathery face, yellow-brown eyes twinkling.

"Damn good to see you again, Mr. Holten."

"I see those stripes stuck, Newcomb," Eli returned as greeting. "A few more years and you can add another one and a rocker."

Grinning wider, if possible, Cpl. Christopher "Kit" Newcomb wrung Eli Holten's hand warmly. "Not unless my Crow scouts get a campaign to work in. Enlisted promotions are harder to come by than officers right now."

"Didn't Colonel Mayberry turn you loose on finding out what happened to Frank Corrington?" Eli asked, suddenly worried.

"Oh, sure. It was one of my boys cut the trail and led the search party to where the prospector said he'd seen the general's body. And we've been out off and on ever since. Thing is, that dog-leg jaspar, Governor Stratton, has told the army to butt out an' Headquarters went along with it."

"What the hell! What happened to Frank is army business, and there's nothing the governonr can do about it."

Newcomb produced a sheepish smile. "That's what Colonel Britton and Lieutenant Colonel Mayberry say. Only the army's not given much stock right now; lot of pressure back East to let the civil authorities handle things. Pretty poems carry more weight than pacifying the tribes. Mr. Lo's ridin' mighty high."

Eli Holten recognized his reference to a popular

eastern newspaper editorial, written in the form of a poem, that extolled the supposed virtues of the Indians. It began, "Lo, the noble savage." The men in the ranks of the frontier army had taken to calling their frequent adversary "Mr. Lo."

"When are we moving out?" Eli asked, changing the subject.

"Soon as those damn mules are hitched. I know they move faster than oxen, but their orneriness outdoes any advantage that gives."

"All right Kit. Get 'em rolling and then you can fill me in on what's been going on."

Newcomb led a detail of five men to escort the dozen wagons which comprised the supply column. Each wagon, Eli found out, had only a driver aboard. The road they took was excellent, being heavily traveled to a point well beyond Fort Rawlins. Once under way, they made good time, able to pitch camp the first night some twenty-five miles west of Pierre. Oxen would have barely made eleven. Holten heard in detail, much lacking in the lurid newspaper accounts, of the unrest and lack of response by the territorial government.

Each revelation fueled a smoldering anger. It also gave credence to his suspicion that Frank Corrington's ambush and attempted murder had a great deal to do with the invasion of Black Hills Treaty land, growing Indian unrest, and the savage raids committed by both sides. With one of the teamsters proving his versatility as a cook, Holten settled down on a bump of rock to sip a cup of middling good coffee. Cpl. Kit Newcomb joined him after posting sentries and inspecting the livestock on the picket line.

"There's no change in the general's condition?" Eli anxiously asked again, as though unwilling to accept the answer.

"None before I left Rawlins," Kit Newcomb informed him.

"How long can he go on like that?"

111

"Don't know, Mr. Holten. That's for the surgeon to decide. Major Jansen don't sound encouraging."

Some sixth sense tickled at the edge of Eli Holten's consciousness. He found it all a bit too much for coincidence. Frank Corrington had been waylaid and left for dead, the territorial government turned a blind eye toward unlawful invasion of Indian-ceded land in the Black Hills, and three ex-convicts, all of whom had been involved in violations in and around the Black Hills in years past, appeared suddenly in Pierre. The possibilities of that combination left him decidedly uneasy.

CHAPTER 11

Suddenly appearing out of a fold in the prairie, a dozen Cheyenne warriors, grim-faced and painted for war, arrayed themselves across the wide trail taken by the Thorne girls. Melissa, on her small gray mare, reined in, with Doreen and Samantha doing likewise with their vehicles. For a long, tense minute, no one spoke. Then little Helen broke the silence.

"OhmyGod," she blurted, running a soft hand over her smooth, high forehead, under the mop of strawberry hair.

Slowly, their desire to spill white blood clear in their eyes, the Cheyenne exchanged glances. The leader kneed his war pony into forward motion. He rode to where Melissa sat her mount. Coldly he examined her, eyes taking in every detail of her lithe, slender body, ample mounds of breasts, long, clean limbs, and thick auburn hair. Melissa wondered nervously why she hadn't taken the basic precaution of riding with her rifle across her lap, a round ready in the chamber.

Over the years on the fringe of the frontier, Melissa and her sisters had picked up enough of the rudiments of the alien language to follow the basic thrust of their conversation. "We come to fight white men, and look what they send us," the leader said through a chuckle.

"The larger two would make good babies," the

warrior on his right observed.

"Ho! Even the little one has that look in her eyes that says she knows what it is like to feel a man deep inside her," a chubby brave with close-set, crossed eyes remarked.

"Do you claim her as your first?" the leader demanded.

Lame Bull rubbed his crotch. "Sure. Why not?" He started his mount forward, moon face aglow. "What do we do after we finish?"

"What else? We kill them," another warrior stated from the group.

Their leader came closer now, then reached out to feel the silky richness of Melissa's hair. An instant later his hand jerked back as though he had burned himself. He leaned forward and peered at Melissa's cleavage.

"This necklace. Where did you get it?" he asked in a mixture of Cheyenne and English.

Melissa's hand went to her throat. Her long, strong fingers touched the bison teeth and beads of her necklace. "It was a gift," she answered. "From a friend, a mighty warrior." She paused, then drew a breath. She could only try. "His name is Eli Holten."

Surprise at recognition of the name robbed the Cheyenne men of their stoic expressions. "See what she wears," the leader informed his men. To Melissa he said, "This is true, what you tell me? This came from Tall Bear of the Oglala, the man Holten?"

Melissa nodded, suddenly afraid to speak. The Cheyenne leader made sign talk in the air. "I am called Spotted Hawk," he added in English. "I am a friend of the Oglala Tall Bear. Describe him so we know you speak truthfully."

Melissa did. Then she added, "He gave it to me nearly four years ago."

Spotted Hawk eyed her closely. "You were his woman then?"

"I . . . was."

Making a sweeping, full-arm gesture to include her sisters, he opened a new subject. "You are so alike, seeds in the same pod."

"We are sisters."

Nodding as though she had imparted a gem of great wisdom, Spotted Hawk considered her words. "Where do you journey?" he asked in his own tongue, translating into English, "Where do you go?"

"Fort Rawlins. To see Eli Holten."

A frown creased Spotted Hawk's coppery brow. "It is a long way, and he is not there."

Disappointment and an edge of icy fear touched Melissa's heart. "Oh, but he must be."

"He is gone long time. Two, nearly three summers."

"Oh, but . . . h-he has to be there to help us."

Spotted Hawk gauged the desperation behind her words and granted her his sympathy in a smile. "These are times of much trouble. His friend, the soldier chief, lies in a sleep, like one dead. Tall Bear will come."

"Y-you're sure of it?" Melissa asked, grasping at faint hope.

"Yes. He has much love in his heart for the soldier chief. He will come." Then he changed the subject. "When you ride, where you go, always wear this necklace. It is powerful medicine, given by Tall Bear; it is also safe conduct. To show that we are friends of Tall Bear, we will ride with you to the edge of the lands of the Sioux."

"My, oh, my—my," Melissa gulped. Would they, she wondered, have to bestow favors, as they had done for the cowboys outside Belle Fourche?"

"Another day and we're at Rawlins," Cpl. Kit Newcomb remarked idly to Eli Holten.

"You needn't mention that I would have been there and had a drink belted down if I'd not poked along with your wagons, Kit."

Newcomb produced a rueful grin. "I figured you had a reason."

"I did. I wanted to get a soldier's eye view of what is going on out here. None of it fits, yet there might be one thread that holds it all together. Do you recall Hezakiah Manning? It would be about five years ago, and he would have been in his mid-thirties. Big, blocky man, with a barrel chest, arms and legs to match, has green eyes, reddish-blond hair?"

"A—ah—whiskey runner, right?"

"That's the one. I saw him in Pierre the day before we left. He was with two other unsavory characters. Amos Wade and Zacharia Walters. They were before your time. The general and I put them in prison for ten years each. Manning got five. Obviously they're out now. Though . . ." Holten let his voice trail off, then picked up his thought. "I don't suppose they have any more reason to get even with Frank than any of fifty or so others. And Manning's more likely to have a hard-on for me than the general."

"Which leads to what?" Newcomb asked ungrammatically.

"Don't get the idea I see dire plots under every rock, Kit. Only, I wonder. If those three had something going that depended upon running the Indians out of the Black Hills altogether and provided an opportunity to revenge themselves on the general and me . . . well, that's all the farther I've gotten. If it sounds like I'm pissing into the wind, tell me so."

Newcomb mulled it over a moment. "Not so's any of the spray would hit me. My only craw-sticker is the same as yours. I can't see what they might be up to."

A moment later they heard the muffled sound of a shot from up ahead. Sonny, Eli's war-trained Morgan stallion, flared his nostrils and shivered loose hide, anxious to get into the battle. Newcomb peered intently to the front. Eli bent on the reins and edged

116

Sonny to the right, clear of the dusty column of wagons.

Away from the squeal and groan of axles and the plodding of mule shoes, Eli heard the rumble of galloping horses. To the west he saw a faint haze of brown smudge. It grew into a pillar of thick dust several seconds before a group of masked men topped a slight swell and raced down toward the wagons. They numbered some twenty, Holten quickly counted. Most waved recent model Winchester repeaters. One man's hat flew off in the wind of their progress. Then puffs of smoke appeared as the trio in the lead opened fire on the caravan.

"Who the hell?" Corporal Newcomb blurted.

Eli had already unlimbered his big Winchester Express rifle and levered a round into the chamber. With Sonny standing as though on parade, Holten aimed from his steady platform and squeezed the trigger. The heavy rifle bellowed, and wind whipped away the cloud of smoke. Satisfaction brought a grin to the scout's lips when he saw a bandit jerk in the saddle and ride a few more paces in a stiffened, unnatural position, then bend sideways and fall from his plunging horse.

"They're not friendly, whoever they are," Eli remarked flippantly.

"Jesus, we don't have a chance stuck out here like this," Corporal Newcomb stated the obvious. "Lash up those teams; bring 'em to a run. We've gotta try to get through them."

Holten fired again, his fat slug splashing into the heaving chest of a galloping horse. The animal folded its legs in mid-stride and plowed up dirt and cactus. The unfortunate rider continued forward in the line of his attack, did a somersault and managed a short, shrill scream before his head made contact with the hard earth and broke his neck. Whips cracked, and the

117

wagons creaked into a minutely faster pace. The drivers cursed and laid on the leather lashes.

With braying protest, the mules leaned into their collars and battled inertia in an attempt to break into a run. Weapons crackled all along the brigand's front. Bullets smacked into wood and screamed off iron wheel rims. A driver grunted and toppled onto his side, a red, wet stain on the back of his shirt. Several teamsters tied off their reins, using their left hands to beleaguer their teams while trading shots with the outlaws with their sidearms.

Sudden as a bolt of lightning, the opposing forces swarmed together. Men shouted and howled. At close quarters, a rifle and sixgun crashed with devastating effect. In the first sweeping dash, two more drivers died before the momentum of the charge carried the outlaws beyond the line of wagons. For a moment, the gunfire ceased. Near the top of the rise, Holten spotted a knobby hill beyond.

Years of scouting in this terrain made him familiar with every feature. There was water there, a seep spring and an easy, shallow ford of the creek it nourished. If they could make it. He lunged forward, spurs goading Sonny to the effort. Waving his hat, he directed the lead teamster in that direction.

"Oh, hell, we can't keep on like this," Corporal Newcomb shouted over the rumble of the wagons.

"Keep pushing them," Eli advised. "We've got to get that hill at our backs. Aim for the ford. Once we're across, it will be easy."

From their rear came a renewed rattle of gunfire. The outlaws charged again. With their firepower reduced by the demands of wagon handling, Corporal Newcomb turned back with Eli Holten and laid down disciplined covering fire that proved too accurate for their attackers.

Their charge broke before it reached the three delivery wagons. When they whirled away, Eli rode to one and mounted, fixing Sonny's reins loosely to the brake lever. Newcomb, a more accomplished wagoneer, rigged a snaffle line from the lead team of one to the front of the other stalled vehicle. Then he, too, traded saddle for driver's seat. They brought the rigs to the ford, side-by-side.

"How much chance do we have?" Newcomb asked anxiously.

Holten had already studied the situation. "Not a hell of a lot. We'll do better with all the wagons. Damn, here they come again. Get across there."

Aiming carefully, Eli knocked down another horse, the rider escaping to be picked up by a companion. One hot round snapped past close to the outlaw leader's head, and the hardcase swung wide, his men following. Holten fired his last round in the Winchester and spilled a man from his saddle. Then he crossed the creek.

"Go ahead," he shouted to Newcomb. "You know what to do."

"Circle the wagons!" Newcomb shouted. He waved his arm to indicate a position that incorporated the steep, knobby hill as a part of their defense and directed the wagons to form a ring at its base.

All too soon after establishing their defensive perimeter, it became apparent to Eli Holten that Fate had turned against the soldiers. He had long been an advocate of the idea that the best way to defend one's self from aggression was to carry the fight to the aggressor. Sitting still and waiting for the enemy to come to one usually resulted in being overwhelmed by that enemy. Yet there was little else that could be done.

Drivers couldn't control their wagons and shoot effectively. They couldn't stop to shoot and cover any ground. They had lost four men so far, one of the five man escort and three drivers. Someone at Fort Rawlins had erred badly. Considering the turmoil in the territory, such a supply detail without at least a matching number of armed troops on the wagons begged to be attacked. Time for blame-placing later, Eli considered as they fought through the waning hours of afternoon.

With the rich prize of the laden supply wagons, the outlaws contented themselves to holding back and engaging in occasional bouts of sniping. They husbanded their ammunition, expending only enough to insure the troopers would not decide to make a run for it.

Sundown found their condition unchanged. At Corporal Newcomb's direction, small, sheltered fires provided a means of cooking a meal. The teamsters, tired from a protracted day of work and fighting, slumped in weary dejection while the escort stood guard.

"Once the drivers are fed," Newcomb commanded, "we'll have you replaced, and the other men will take the watch through the night."

"I might try slipping out of here and going for help," Holten suggested.

"You could, but by the time you reached Rawlins and returned, we'd be faded memories for our families to treasure."

"Hey, you! Soldier boys," a voice called out of the darkness. "We know you have Eli Holten with you. All we really want is him. Send out the scout and the rest of you can go on your way."

"In a pig's ass," Newcomb growled back at them.

"No—no, we mean it. We got no quarrel with you. No sense in our getting each other shot up for nothing. Give us Holten and you can keep right on to the fort."

"Go fu—" Newcomb cut off his words when Eli grabbed one arm and shook his head violently, frowning.

"Don't slam the door to a possible way out of this," the scout said quietly. "Say nothing now. They'll figure you're thinking it over, maybe deciding among you.

Whether he's telling the truth or not, they seem more interested in getting at me than in fighting it out for possession of the supplies and wagons. While we make them sweat for it, I've got an idea how we can use this to advantage."

Al Hardy rolled a perfect cigarette one-handed, twisted the ends and lighted it with a twig from the edge of the fire pit. Al was well pleased with himself. Five men, outfitted with army uniforms, were on the way to Fort Rawlins to deal with General Corrington. When he learned that Eli Holten had left Pierre with the supply detail, he had acted at once. With Amos Wade's blessing, he dispatched ten men to scout the route to the fort while he followed with ten more.

Early that morning the two elements had joined. Al learned that the wagons were guarded by only six men, plus Eli Holten. It would all be so easy. He would collect Holten's scalp and have the profit from the wagons as well. Then they had met more resistance than expected. A couple of mistakes and a weak point in the line let the caravan slip through and laager up at Bald Knob, across Spiney Creek. For a while there, Al thought they might lose the whole venture.

Then reinforcements arrived, another eight of his regular crew. Nightfall had found the situation unchanged for the soldiers. He had pickets out to make sure none of the troopers decided to make a break to get help. Al and his men had eaten well. They would get a good night's rest. Then, in the morning, they would finish off Eli Holten and haul the wagons off to convert the supplies to cash. That would leave only that meddlesome general to deal with, and he had confidence in the men he sent to handle that.

"Granger, Owens," Al summoned as he rose to pour more coffee into his tin cup. "Go out and check on the boys. Make sure they don't fall asleep. We don't want any of those so'jers sneakin' off and getting help."

"Right enough," Granger agreed.

From a saddle notch between two hills to the north, a coyote gave voice to pent-up passion. The ululating wail echoed off the dead end the army wagons had been driven against. A thin sliver of waxing moon provided scant, frosty light to the rolling pairie to the south and east. Al Handy took a deep drag on his cigarette and snapped the butt into the fire. Without guidance, his hand sought out the makins, and he started to roll another smoke.

Al touched his tongue to the wheat-straw paper a moment before an owl hooted in a cottonwood by the creek, beyond the end of their left flank. Al's index finger slicked down the cigarette's seam, and his confidence soared. Another owl, downstream to the right, made mournful music, answered at once by the one to the north. Al yawned and stretched, took a long drag and flipped his half-smoked quirley into the pulsing coals.

Smiling to himself, Al headed for his blankets. The owl hooted again.

Dawn increased the tensions inside the ring of wagons. Lacking a wood supply, the soldiers could not prepare coffee or cook any food. The odor of frying bacon and brewing coffee wafted over from the outlaw camp to torment the troopers. With the coming of light, the men of Brigade Headquarters faced a new trial.

"You boys hungry?" a taunting voice called from across the creek.

"Hey, fellers, the coffee's great. C'mon over and have some."

"You so'jers are sure dumb. All you gotta do is hand over Eli Holten and you can go on your own way."

"That's right," Al Handy's baritone agreed. "Give up

Holten and you can still make the fort before evening chow. It's up to you. We've got bacon and beans over here, with cornbread and lots of coffee. And we've got all the time in the world. What d'ya say?"

"Lay off, will you?" Private Dennis called in an aggrieved voice. "We're thinkin' on it."

"We are like hell," Corporal Newcomb roared. "Keep it buttoned up, Dennis."

"Hell with this, Newcomb," another soldier complained. "My arm aches where I got nicked yesterday. Keep this up and it'll 'nfect, and I'll lose it."

Ei Holten appeared in the magnified circle of the field glasses Al Handy held to his eyes. He led his big black by the reins, all saddled and ready. He and the corporal in charge appeared to be arguing over something. Their gestures became more agitated, and voices rose until Al could hear clearly.

"It's me they're after, Newcomb. Don't be a fool. I've got a better chance on my own than staying here and forcing a fight."

"Now dammit, Mr. Holten, that's an unnecessary risk. You've no call to ride over there and risk bein' killed."

"It's my life."

Several soldiers had gathered around by now. They began to argue with Newcomb and gesture pointedly across the creek in Al's direction. Two of them stepped between Newcomb and Holten, and another big, brawny trooper took the scout by one elbow and pulled him toward the Morgan's side. Grim expressions abounded among the soldiers. Al's face split in a huge grin.

The smirk remained on his lips as Holten was handed the reins and turned his horse toward the ford. Al wanted to dance a little jig. Everything was going his way.

CHAPTER 12

A brown thrasher warbled from the hilltop, saluting Handy's victory, as the hardcase saw it. Another answered from beyond the line of waiting outlaws to the north. Eli Holten rode stiffly, as though expecting a bullet at any moment. His big Morgan stallion daintily picked out a path between the rocks and scattered gear to the ring of wagons. Two troopers picked up a wagon tongue, and Holten walked his mount out into the open.

"We knew you'd see it our way!" Handy couldn't resist the taunt.

In a flash, things stopped going Al Handy's way. Eli Holten dug spurs into Sonny's flanks and streaked toward the crest of the saddle, well beyond the northern flank of the outlaw position. Sparkling, fist-sized blobs of water flew high into the air as he plunged across the creek above the ford. For a moment he disappeared into a fringe of willows. Several rifles barked in anger.

Lacking a positive target, the bullets went stray. Then Holten appeared again, beyond the low, drooping trees, his Morgan in full gallop. "Get after him!" Al barked.

Three outlaws ran to their waiting horses. Two more dashed for theirs. With a fading rumble, the scout continued to put distance between them. A glance ahead showed him some three hundred yards to go. Bent low, Eli spoke softly into his mount's right ear.

"Keep goin', boy. That's it, Sonny, give me all you've got."

Behind him, men shouted curses, and a rifle cracked. The bullet gouged up dirt fifty feet to one side of the fleeing Holten. Straining into a steeper incline, Holten wasted no ammunition on return fire. Wind stung his eyes and caused them to tear. He wiped at the moisture with his gloved right hand. Sonny's haunches churned, and his forequarters rolled with effort. Nearing the top at last, Holten hazarded a glance backward.

Less than two hundred yards separated him from the pursuing outlaws. They would slow, he knew, when they reached the steeper grade, yet their present gain introduced a thread of doubt. Had his gamble failed? Had he and Newcomb acted out their little farce for nothing? Blue sky suddenly filled all space before him in a dazzling arc. He'd made it so far.

Sonny plunged over the saddle notch, bearing Holten out of sight of his pursuers. Eli looked up in time to yank hard on the reins. Sonny set his hind hoofs and stopped a yard short of crashing into a line of grim-faced Cheyenne warriors. Swift enlightenment washed over the scout.

In the wan light of the previous night, Eli had heard and recorded in his mind the animal and bird calls. Automatically he cataloged them as having come from human throats. Indians, of course. Hunters? Perhaps. A war party? From what he had been hearing, that seemed more likely. The bold fires of the outlaw band would have attracted them. They would have checked out a potential enemy before moving along. He had no idea at the time, no shining inspiration, that they might remain behind to determine the outcome of the obvious confrontation. For what purpose? Maybe to clean up the victorious survivors? One face, at the center of the arc of warriors, resolved into recognition for the scout. For the moment it relaxed him.

"Ho, Mahto Tanka running away from a fight?" the familiar Cheyenne greeted in jest, speaking Lakota.

"Heoka, Spotted Hawk, are you hiding here from the same enemy? It must be or you would have attacked last night."

Spotted Hawk raised an eyebrow. "You knew we were here?"

"I saw and heard some of you in the night. It gave me reason to believe that more of my Cheyenne cousins might be close by."

A nod of acknowledgement answered him. Spotted Hawk spoke to his subordinates. "Brush away those flies," he commanded.

Half a dozen war-painted Cheyenne slipped from their mounts and went toward the crest of the saddle, rifles in hand. They took good positions and began to fire at the unsuspecting outlaws. Holten and Spotted Hawk exchanged smiles.

"Why have you bothered with a fight between white men?" Holten asked.

Spotted Hawk gestured with his rifle. "The men who attack your wagons are the same we want for the murder of our women and children."

A rush of rifle fire and the twang of two bowstrings announced the arrival of the pursuing outlaws. Holten and Spotted Hawk rode forward to watch. Expressions of surprise and terror could be plainly read on the suddenly pale faces of the hardcases. Expecting to find one fleeing man, they found themselves in a deadly trap, bullets and arrows flying all around. Two turned off at once, racing away downhill.

Each of the other three discharged his weapon once. Then one screamed in terrible agony as two arrows pierced his belly. The head of one projectile protruded from his back, in the region of his right kidney. Two slugs slapped meat in another bandit. He yanked violently on the reins and upset his horse. Immediately a youth in his early teens rushed out to retrieve the animal, ignoring the man who lay kicking feebly in his death throes. The remaining outlaw gave a "what the hell" shrug and charged his ambushers.

His horse made three loping strides forward before five hot slugs slammed into the man's torso. Bleeding profusely, he fell from the saddle, and another youngster of thirteen or so ran to capture his mount.

"They are your enemies, too?" Holten remarked offhandedly.

"Yes."

"Well, then, what's keeping you?"

Eager to finish it, Al Handy ordered an immediate attack on the unsuspecting wagons. He had no intention of letting so rich a prize escape. When his men reached the creek, he discovered that the army teamsters weren't as trusting as he expected. A flaming volley from .45-70 Springfields rippled across the front wall of wagons. His men flinched back, two down wounded and screaming. In the silence that followed the fusillade, he heard the rattle of gunfire from the saddle notch.

At least something had gone right, Al considered. That had to be the end of Eli Holten. Now to finish off the soldiers. He waved his men forward again.

"Get moving. We don't have all day."

Handy's hardcases made it to mid-stream before the troopers fired another volley. Horses, spooked by the rushing water, reared and threatened to unsaddle their rides. Men yelled and cursed. Half a dozen returned the army's fire. Then one of his men toward the end of the right flank let out a frightened cry.

"Indians! Jesus Christ, there must be a hunnard

127

Cheyenne comin' this way."

Eli Holten, at the head of twenty screaming, painted warriors, thundered over the saddle notch and down on the astonished outlaws. Swiftly the range closed, so that Al Handy and his men became trapped between two hostile forces. The volume of fire increased from the soldiers, lashing at the huddled bandits. Of the twenty-five remaining, three died just moments after the frightened announcement.

"Swing wide," Holten yelled in the Cheyenne tongue. "Cut off any escape."

"Stiff Leg, take eight men," Spotted Hawk added.

With the range rapidly closing, Eli Holten scabbarded his Winchester and drew the conversion model Remington Army revolver. For a while, targets abounded. Holten and the Cheyenne and the soldiers might as well have been at a shooting gallery. Handy's reinforcements did him little good. They died like the rest. Howling fiercely, the Cheyenne leaped from their ponies to finish off any wounded who fell nearby.

"We gotta get out of here," Burt Sands shouted directly in Al Handy's ear.

Recovered enough from the awful surprise to use his wits, Al made a quick assessment of the situation. "Head south. Stay in the creek and we can ride around the wagons."

Handy and two men jumped their horses into a splashing trot away from the swirling violence. Holten noted their fleeing backs, yet found himself unable to disengage and go after them. A screaming, fat outlaw came at him, a short-barreled shotgun held one-handed. Eli saw the muzzles lining up on his chest and kicked his right foot free of the stirrup. In the same instant the hammer fell, he flung himself to the left and forward to cling to Sonny's neck.

A loud roar battered his ears, and he levered himself

up enough to see the shotgunner crowd past. Sixgun still in his grip, Eli took slanting aim and squeezed the trigger. The Remington bucked in his hand, and a red-splashed hole appeared in the side of the outlaw's head.

The man dropped the shotgun and slumped forward on the neck of his nervous, sweating horse. The far side of his head had been blown away, and the man beside him, splattered with bits of the gore, began to gag and retch. Holten regained his saddle and shot the vomiting man in a beefy shoulder joint. Suddenly another outlaw appeared at the edge of the red haze of Eli's battle lust.

With a quick jerk of his arm, Eli started to line up on the bandit, only to realize that the man had his arms high above his head. He was surrendering. Three more shots sounded. An arrow made its death-song hum through the air, and another outlaw died in screaming agony. Then a terrible silence came over the badly churned, blood-soaked ground. Eli Holten looked around.

Relentlessly the Cheyenne warriors walked among the fallen. Here and there one would bend, cut a throat, take a scalp. Holten turned away, to find Corporal Kit Newcomb headed his way from the laager. Ahead of him marched two crestfallen prisoners.

"They saw what your friends were doing," Newcomb explained, "and threw themselves on our mercy. I had a mind to toss 'em out for the Cheyenne."

"Y-you couldn't do that; you're a white man," one of the captives whimpered.

Holten gave him an icy stare. "*I* can. And I will if you don't tell me everything you know about this attack. Who planned it, what's behind it and a whole lot more I want to know."

"You can't make us talk," his fellow prisoner sneered.

Holten looked at him as though seeing something of his sort for the first time. "Do you have a hearing problem? I just said I would turn you over to the Cheyenne. See that one there, the tall, barrel-chested one with the three eagle feathers in his hair? He's a war chief. His name is Spotted Hawk. He says you and these other men attacked his village, murdered their wives and children, the old people. They're killing the wounded now. Do you have any idea what they might do with someone unharmed and able to endure prolonged torture?"

Younger and thoroughly intimidated, the other hardcase licked dry lips and spoke with a broken voice. "You're Eli Holten, aren't you?"

"That's right."

"They say you lived with the Sioux. They called you Tall Bear."

"Right again. The Oglala. Two Bulls was my adoptive father. When I was your age, I rode with the Oglala as a warrior, killing Crow and Arakaree. I saw the Sioux skin a man alive one time. Surprisingly he lived five days afterward. He did a lot of screaming though."

"Jesus, Mr. Holten, nobody co-co-could turn a fellow white man over to th-those savages."

Holten worked up a smile of utter nastiness. "I just told you, I am an Oglala, named Tall Bear. I don't give a damn what they do to you."

Eli's last word had barely left his lips when the youthful captive lost control of his bladder. The older two sneered and ridiculed him. What they said didn't matter. By the time he finished telling all he knew, Eli Holten had a far better idea of what had been going on.

Sated on the killing already completed, the Cheyenne warriors let the army have the three prisoners. They would be interrogated further at Fort Rawlins. When the wagons started up again, the scout appeared somewhat distracted. He no longer had any doubt that Amos Wade and his low-life friends had formulated all of the trouble, including the attempt on Frank

Corrington's life. What kept him detached from his surroundings was a hard effort to formulate some plan that would catch the conspirators in a manner that would let the army deal with them, instead of the civil authorities. That offered better than even odds that they would not come out of it alive.

"I'm glad you got here," Lieutenant Colonel Mayberry told Eli Holten, wringing the scout's hand. "The situation gets worse every day, and we can't do anything about it."

"How is Frank?" Eli asked, tense and anxious over the answer.

"He's still unconscious. But he's become restless. That's a good sign, the doctor says. We'll go over there in a little while. Now tell me, what about this outlaw attack on the way here?"

Eli adjusted his position on the straight-back chair he occupied. He wished ever so much for a shot of Frank Corrington's good brandy before beginning. As though reading his mind, Lieutenant Colonel Mayberry spoke again.

"I have some excellent bourbon here, Jack Daniels from Tennessee. Can I interest you in a little?" His humorous, knowing smile implied he knew the answer.

Holten accepted the glass and peered deeply into the dark amber liquid. "What do you mean, it's worse and you can't do anything about it?"

Quickly Mayberry filled him in on the situation with Department Headquarters and the territorial government. He concluded with a shrug and a heavy sigh. "So, we sit here on our hands, watching the tribes work themselves and each other up into a general uprising, while the governor does nothing about the treaty breakers."

For a moment, Eli hesitated in lecturing an officer of such considerable experience as Howard Mayberry.

131

Then he downed half his bourbon and delivered the words Mayberry had been silently praying to hear.

"Howard, the primary responsibility for maintaining the peace and security of the frontier lies with the army. There is nothing and no one who can prevent you from accomplishing your mission. Hell, you know all this. Are you sending out patrols?"

"Some," Mayberry answered tentatively.

"Send out more. Larger ones, say company strength. Have Sam Britton put the infantry on the move, march and countermarch, establish outposts. If in the process they discover violations, it's their duty to deal with them."

"Governor Stratton will have fits. He'll complain to St. Paul."

"Fuck the governor and that flock of nitwits that hangs around him," Holten growled. "I may sound like a guardhouse lawyer, Howard, but one fact takes precedent over all the rest. No one can issue orders, and make them stick, for you not to fulfill your assigned duties without the consent of the commanding officer of the Division of the Missouri, and ultimately the War Department. Bill Sherman isn't going to give such an order. Somehow, Governor Stratton has gotten to General Pickering. You know the old saw, 'If you can't dazzle them with details, blind them with bullshit.'

"I think it's time to get back to business as usual, and I think Frank would say the same thing." Holten paused and downed the rest of his Jack Black, then held out the glass for more.

Lieutenant Colonel Mayberry produced a sardonic chuckle while he poured. "I'm sure he would. But there's enormous pressure from back East. The nation has to expand. The press alone—"

"Ah, yes, the splendid gentlemen of the press. Give me a week in the field with all the representatives of the eastern press, and I'll show them things that will curl their toes. It all boils down to this, Howard. If you are

132

doing your job, according to *standing* orders, and you happen to come upon treaty violators, no secondary order from a department commander, without higher authority, can prevent you from acting on the situation. The final judgement of what is necessary and proper rests with the *commander in the field.*"

Mayberry beamed, his eyes alight for the first time since Eli Holten arrived. His bitter tone dissolved into a rich, mellow baritone, tinged with anticipation. "By damn, you're right. I knew that all along. I suppose I just wanted to hear someone else say it. I'll get Sergeant Major Childers on cutting a patrol schedule right away. Sam'll love it, too."

A knock at the door intruded. Sergeant Major Childers opened the portal a crack and announced, "Messenger from the dispensary, sir."

"Send him in," Mayberry snapped.

A young private, in hospitalman's white, entered and stamped to the desk, to halt and deliver a precise salute. "Hospitalman Johnson, sir. The post surgeon's compliments, sir, and will you come immediately. General Corrington is regaining consciousness."

"By God, that's good news. Thank you, Hospitalman. We'll come at once."

"That goddamned Holten," Lamar Owens growled. "He'n the army will squeeze everything out of us if they get the chance."

Due to the overpopulation of cells, as a result of inactivity, the trio of hardcases captured at the Spinney Creek fight had been locked up together. Their wounds tended by Major Jansen, the three men sat on two lower bunks in the stockade cellblock discussing their situation.

"I don't intend to allow them the time," Carl Brauer spat.

"Oh?" Owens sneered. "What do you intend to do?

133

Walk through that fucking wall?"

Brauer grunted and shifted position on the thin, straw-filled mattress. "Something like that. It's plain fact, we've got to get the hell outta here. We couldn't have a better time than right now."

"Wo-won't they shoot us?" the youngest hardcase asked hesitantly.

"Not if we do it right," Brauer assured him. "No one would expect wounded men to try anything. Hell, they never even put on extra guards. So what we have to do is figger a way to get that turnkey in here and us out."

"Then what?" the dubious youth prompted.

"We get to the stable, grab horses and go out through the water gate, behind the corrals."

"I don't know, Carl. Sounds mighty risky to me," the uncertain youth protested.

"You already spilled your guts. All life's a risk, kid. You're either with us or we leave you here . . . dead. Now what'll it be?"

"All—all right, I'll go."

Brauer produced a yellowed, broken-tooth grin. "Good. Now, here's what we'll do . . ."

CHAPTER 13

"Hey, guard—guard!" Lamar Owens yelled. "The kid here's bleedin' bad. That bandage the doc put on him didn't do much good. Hurry, man, he's gonna bleed to death."

"Guard, hurry, man. He's all pale and shaking," Carl Brauer added. "Bring the turnkey and a hospitalman."

A key rattled at the far end of the cellblock. "Yeah, yeah, keep a lid on it. I'm coming."

Metal shrieked dryly as the steel door pins turned in the hinges. A moment later, the turnkey came into view. "Stop that ruckus. I'll have him out of there and over to dispensary. You two, move back."

After entering the cell, the turnkey bent over the bunk where the young outlaw lay, his body quaking as though in a deep chill. The garrison soldier lifted the apparently ill man, only to have him slump back.

"Here, I'll help," Carl Brauer blurted disarmingly as he stepped forward.

His arm looped around the trooper's neck and squeezed his larynx. Yanked backward, the turnkey struggled uselessly against the hold, his feet off the floor. Quickly Lamar Owens grabbed the key ring. His balled fist struck the guard at the exact point on his jawline with a soft smack.

Eyes rolled back, the turnkey went slack. "Lay him

on the bunk," Owens commanded. "Let's get out of here."

In the guard room, they found the stockade sentries gone to early chow. Owens and Brauer armed themselves from the rack of weapons behind the guard sergeant's desk. The desperate trio rushed to the door as one man. Owens opened it a crack and surveyed the empty parade ground beyond.

No one stirred, and none looked in the direction of the stockade. Sighing with relief, Owens flung the door wide, and they burst into the open. Wordlessly Brauer pointed toward the distant stables. The three hardcases started a shambling run across the corner of the parade ground. At the same moment, Eli Holten, accompanied by Lieutenant Colonel Mayberry, stepped out of the headquarters building. A quick glance over his left shoulder revealed Holten to Carl Brauer.

"Lamar, it's Holten. Now's our chance." Brauer halted and brought up his stolen Smith & Wesson Scoffield .45.

Brauer's shot echoed off the buildings and palisades, making the task of locating the source difficult. He eared back the hammer as Holten drew his Remington. A light breeze blew the elongated puff of powder smoke across the parade.

"Come on, come on," Lamar Owens urged, yanking at Brauer's left arm.

"I'm gonna get him. I'm gonna kill that bastard Holten," the would-be assassin shouted. He fired again, and Eli Holten felt the wind of the slug's passage as it cracked past his head. Something tugged at his right earlobe, and sharp, clear pain erupted in Eli's head.

Before the white ball of agony robbed him of sight, Eli triggered another round. Automatically he began to cock his Remington, a short gasp came from his lips, then the parade ground swam into view once more.

Carl Brauer had gone down on one knee. An oozing

spread of crimson stained his shirtfront. In seemingly slow motion, Brauer raised the purloined revolver and clumsily thumbed back the hammer. Biting his lower lip, conscious of a warm, sticky flow along his neck, Eli Holten lined his eye and front sight on Brauer's chest, and his index finger tripped the hammer.

A puff of red-tinged dust and powdered cloth rose from the left side of Brauer's chest, and he rocked backward. He appeared to have caught himself for a moment; then reaction set in, and he slung the .45 Scoffield high in the air and flopped forward on his face. Blubbering in terror, the young outlaw beside him threw himself on the ground, hands high in the air.

"Don't shoot! Please, don't shoot me," he shrieked, all mannerisms of a frontier tough abandoned.

Lamar Owens tried to run for it. Steadying himself, Eli Holten took careful aim. The fat, 250 grain slug from his .44 Remington ripped through flesh, cartilage and bone from the back of Owens' left knee. His feet went out from under him, and he flopped in the dirt, his face only inches from a litter of fresh, odorous horse dung.

"I want to save him for a little friendly questioning," Eli explained to a gape-mouthed Howard Mayberry.

"That whole thing didn't take a minute," Lieutenant Colonel Mayberry stammered. He looked closely at the scout for the first time since Brauer's initial shot. "He clipped your right earlobe. We'll get that doctored right away."

"Nope. Let me have your neck scarf. We'll see Frank, then have it taken care of," Holten insisted.

The 12th Cavalry's commander prevailed. Major Johnson dabbed and sewed and applied a bandage, all the while complaining about the inconsideration of some of his patients. Then the medico led the way to General Frank Corrington's room.

Frank Corrington looked like Old Man Death, Eli

137

thought as he loooked at the wasted figure on the starched white bed. He and Mayberry entered quietly, behind Major Jansen. Moving like an old man, Frank Corrington turned his head and peered through slitted eyelids at his visitors.

"Eli?" It came out a croak.

Holten's heart ached. Inured to privation, disease, carnage and death, Eli still found himself unable to remain dispassionate in the face of what had happened to Frank Corrington. He wanted to shout, to rage, to hit something. With a powerful force of will, he regained control of his rampant emotions.

"What happened to you, Frank?" Not so bad. Not even a quaver.

"I got the hell beat out of me. What does it look like?"

"Took a couple of bullets, too, I hear." So far his voice reached his ears smooth, even, his usual self.

"That's what this pill-roller tells me," Corrington remarked with an improving conversational tone. "What's got you so worried, Eli? I'm awake and nearly mended."

So much for his spritely bedside manner. "I left Arizona nine days ago. At that time you were almost dead."

"I'm too mean to die, you know that, Eli."

"Frank . . ." Holten made a helpless gesture. "Do—do you feel up to talking about it?"

"Of course. If I had a brandy and a cigar I would."

"Oh, no. Absolutely not. I forbid it, ah, begging the general's pardon, sir," Major Jansen insisted.

"Coffee, then," Lieutenant Colonel Mayberry suggested.

"Yes. Coffee for you gentlemen, clear broth for the general," Jansen insisted.

An orderly was summoned and sent off to fill the order. Holten and Mayberry took chairs, with the doctor hovering around like a mother hen. They remarked on the full bloom of spring and General Corrington observed that he had vague flashes of a snow storm before his final blackout. Once the beverages had been distributed, the general cleared his throat and launched into a narrative that grew disjointed as he progressed.

"I received a message that stated the author knew something about a conspiracy between members of the territorial government and some unsavory characters to violate the Black Hills Treaties with the Indians and exploit the resourccs of the region for their mutual profit. It named a place to meet and that I was to come alone, of course." Corrington broke off his narrative to sip the broth and move about uncomfortably.

"Can you prop up these pillows so that I can see who I'm talking to?" When Major Jansen had completed that, he continued. "Thank you, Major. Now, where was I? Oh, the message. Needless to say, I didn't go alone. I didn't reveal the purpose of the expedition, said I wanted to get in a little hunting. Once we got out a ways, I contrived to get separated from the detail. I didn't figure we'd be far enough apart to be out of hearing range of a gunshot, in case something went wrong. Anyway, I went on to the rendezvous point.

"They jumped me there. A group of a dozen white men. I recognized one, Al Handy. Two of them held me while the rest beat the hell out of me. Then Handy pushed right up in my face and said, 'This is for Amos Wade, Zack Walters and Hezakiah Manning.' Then they shot me and left me for dead." General Corrington sighed and shivered slightly, his scant color draining momentarily. Major Jansen popped to his side, solicitous though abrupt.

"I think that is entirely enough, gentlemen," he decreed.

"No—no, it's all right. I can get the rest out. It's not much. After they left, no during the beating, it began to snow. It might be subjective, but to me it seemed the temperature dropped thirty degrees in less than half an hour after they rode off. By then a man couldn't see ten feet in front of himself because of the swirling snow. I kept blacking out, two, three, maybe four times. Once when I came around it had stopped snowing. I'd been completely covered. It took all my strength to clear some of it away so that I could breathe clearly. Then I dropped off and it snowed again. Later, sometime, I remember an old man's voice, muttering to himself about finding me. Then . . . nothing until I woke up this morning."

"You're sure, Frank?" Eli Holten asked. "It was Al Handy? And he mentioned Wade, Walters and Manning?"

"Y-yes. Of that much I am positive."

"Please, gentlemen, this has to come to an end," a worry-creased Major Jansen demanded.

"No, please. Just a minute more. It's important. Frank, here's what I stumbled across on the way here." Speaking rapidly, Eli filled the general in on his encounter with Al Handy's gang, the glimpse of Wade and his cronies in Pierre, and the state of disaffection among the tribes. He summed up with his absolute certainty, based on what the general had said, that Wade, Walters and Manning, along with Handy, masterminded the entire explosive chain of events.

General Corrington placed a gnarled, illness-withered hand on Eli's solid forearm. "Take the Twelfth, Eli, and ride those bastards down."

"B-but, General, sir," Lieutenant Colonel Mayberry protested. "Headquarters has given specific orders not to do harm to, or to intervene in the activities of the white civilians in the Black Hills."

"Fuck Headquarters," Frank Corrington snapped, his voice resonant with his former vitality.

Grins bloomed on the faces of Eli Holten and Howard Mayberry, and they exchanged nods of knowing satisfaction. They said their good-byes and promised to return when the doctor would let them. Outside the dispensary, Lieutenant Colonel Mayberry could no longer contain himself.

"I told you, Eli. I knew he'd say the same thing you did. But I had to wait and hear it first. Now we start kicking some outlaw ass."

Headquarters Trumpeter, Corporal Sven Aarnsen, took the mouthpiece of his instrument from his lips while the last golden note of *Officers' Call* still echoed across the parade ground. Brigade staff and those of each regiment filed into the appointed rooms. A note from the Reverend Hershel Sommers, sent to Colonel Britton, had been copied and was dutifully read to each gathering of officers.

"I regret to inform you," it read in part, "that the Sioux young men are leaving this agency to join with their Cheyenne cousins in punative actions against the trespassers in the Black Hills. Communication with other agencies verifies that this is also happening throughout the region of the Upper Missouri and the Platte. The entire military Department of Dakota and the western half of the Department of the Platte are involved. There is general, open talk among those who remain on reservations of a new alliance of the tribes, likened unto that which existed in 1875-76, this time for the express purpose of driving the whites from the Black Hills. My Indian police have advised me of the presence of visiting emissaries from tribes as far distant as the Shoshoni and Utes, the Kiowa and Comanches. The results of such a confederation would be nothing less than disastrous. It is my considered opinion that in the best interests of the United States of America, the army must act decisively, and at once, regardless of prior restraints placed upon it by civil authority."

Excited murmurs, ranging from consternation to bellicosity, went around the length of each set of jammed together tables. In the room allocated to the 12th U.S. Cavalry, Lieutenant Colonel Howard Mayberry rose from his chair behind the "T" shaped head of the conference table. He exchanged a quick glance with Eli Holten before he began.

"Gentlemen, you all know that General Corrington has returned to consciousness, if not to duty, with his reason intact. At his precise order, to act decisively and at once is exactly what the Twelfth is going to do."

Several shouts of approbation rang around the room. After quick assurance of consensus among brother officers, all faces turned back expectantly to the commanding officer.

"Standard preparations for going into the field will commence following Officers' Call. Draw rations and fodder enough for an extended campaign of thirty days. All furloughs are here-by cancelled, and any personnel currently on leave from post are to be recalled. Personal issue of ammunition is to be doubled to sixty rounds per man. Troops are to be outfitted and ready for departure at eight o'clock tomorrow morning."

"How are we going to work this, Colonel?" Captain Thompson of Company B inquired.

"Once we reach the area of operation, which begins thirty miles west of the fort, company-sized patrols will be sent out to the north and south of the line of march to a distance of forty miles. One day's ride, gentlemen. Picket posts will be established for the purpose of relaying messages. Any Indians found off the reservations are to be rounded up and escorted to the proper agencies and restrained in the stockades when necessary. Housekeeping troops at the Rose Bud, Pine Ridge and the other agencies can handle that. When we reach the Black Hills, all interlopers uncovered on treaty land will be forcibly removed. There will be no exceptions. Continuing our advance, we will encounter any remaining hostiles and inform them of our actions and send them back where they belong. In the event of any resistance, the hostiles will be disarmed and returned under guard. When this portion of the mission is completed, another sweep of treaty lands in the Black Hills will be made. If any of the following named men are encountered, they are to be arrested and brought here for transportation to St. Paul for trial by military tribunal at Fort Snelling. Amos Wade, Zacharia Walters, Hezakiah Manning, Albert Handy, also known as Bitter Root Al, and . . ." Lieutenant Colonel Howard Mayberry paused before dropping his shocker on his officers. "Governor Delevan Stratton."

Thirty miles west of Fort Rawlins, the Thorne sisters wended their way toward the mecca of their dreams. Melissa, Samantha, Susanna and Helen rode horseback. Doreen drove the buckboard. Along the trail the cart had broken a wheel, and they had been forced to abandon it. Its team had been converted to pack animals, led by the twins. Little Helen had a dapplegray gelding, her favorite, which had once been tied to the tailgate of the wagon. They had long since parted with the Cheyenne warriors. Their bright and expectant faces had been altered into the pinched expressions of those on the edge of despair.

"How much farther do we have?" Helen asked querulously.

At first she had taken the usual pleasure out of riding bareback astride the little gray. She would ride for hours, her eyes glazed and her breath in short, gulping pants that inexorably grew more frequent and pronounced until they crescendoed and the process started over again. Now her crotch was sore. The inner

143

surfaces of her thighs remained permanently red, the flesh abraded and muscles stretched. When dismounted she walked, by her own inventive admission, like a "woman who had birthed twin watermelons."

"Two, three days," Melissa advised in a bored tone.

"Are you sure he's gonna be there? Them Cheyenne said he didn't work for the army any more. Least not at Fort Rawlins," Helen pressed.

"Honey, he's got to be," her eldest sister cried.

"I'll never forget him, never, so long as I live," Doreen cooed.

"Not me," Samantha added. "Nor me," Susanna mooned.

Melissa giggled. With nothing else to pass the endless hours, memories filled the moments. "Remember the time we had him in the tub? You shed your dress, Doreen, and got in astraddle of him. He was so relaxed you sat down on about half of that marvelous machine of his before his eyes popped open."

Doreen produced a trill of laughter. "Oh, don't I just know it. I thought his eyes would bug right outten his head."

"How about the time," the twins said in unison, then Samantha continued alone, "when Susie an' me took opposite sides of him and set to pesterin' that one-eyed snake like kittens lappin' cream."

"Or when we four were all in bed with him, takin' turns, and Helen caught Peter an' Paul peekin' through a chink in the wall and poundin' their puds. Poor li'l Paul was so scared he couldn't get it up for a week."

"I recollect the last time," Susanna said wistfully. "What a wonderful time we all had. We'uns wound up sore as an unlanced boil, like always, and cryin' 'cause we couldn't take on more."

"Why can't y'all shut up!" Helen exploded. "It ain't fair," she complained. "Y'all have had so many more chances to pleasure yourselves with his divine dingus an'—an' I've only gotten to it once. Now you go

144

pesterin' me about all the good times until I itch and crawl till I want to howl to the moon."

"That 'once' was all day," Susanna said cattily.

Melissa took pity on her younger sister. "Soon," she assured Helen. "Soon we'll all have our fill of him. Soon we'll all five be rolling in the field of delight with that paragon of manly pleasure, Eli Holten."

CHAPTER 14

Night settled over Fort Rawlins like a comfortable old blanket. Sentries walked their posts and called out their observations when required by the Corporal of the Guard. With the entire brigade on alert, no one had passed beyond the tall, double front gates, which had been closed at sunset. At nine-twenty, the rattle of wagon wheels attracted the guard on the walkway above the main entrance.

"Corporal of the Guard, Post Number Two!" his alert went out.

Corporal Flannigan of Headquarters Company came out of the guardhouse, sliding his suspenders onto thick, powerful shoulders. "What is it, soldier?"

"A wagon and outriders approaching, Corporal."

"How many men?" Flannigan inquired as ritual required.

"Two—three riders, I count four with the driver, Corporal. Ah, it's an army ambulance, Corporal Flannigan."

"Well don't stand there, ladies, let's get ready to receive them," the corporal growled.

Remembering his general orders, *"I will challenge all persons on or near my post,"* Private Reed brought his Springfield to port arms and bellowed into the darkness. "Halt. Who goes there?"

146

"Friend," came the answer as the lead rider entered the circle of yellow light from flambeaus mounted to either side of the main gate. "We have an injured man from Ten Sleeps outpost. He's got a broke leg needs to be set right."

Sergeant stripes showed yellow on the speaker's sleeve. "Uh . . . just a minute, Sergeant. Corporal Flannigan?"

"Open the gate," Flannigan commanded.

Four men hurried from where they lounged away their duty hours in the gate house. Two swung the huge crossbar while the other pair pulled the stop pins. Heaving, they dragged the fir log gates open. Iron tires grating on the dirt, the ambulance rattled into the fort. Immediately the four soldiers closed and secured the gate. The ambulance went directly to the dispensary.

There the usual bustle and chatter rose around the arrival of an injured soldier. One of the orderlies trotted off toward Officers' Row to inform Major Jansen. The others stood around in anticipation, though feeling useless, while the men accompanying the vehicle unloaded a stretcher. The man on it groaned at the rough handling.

"Get him inside," the senior hospitalman growled for want of something to do.

"Right away," the sergeant responded, mustache elevated by a smug grin.

Hez Manning had felt uneasy about the plan to infiltrate Fort Rawlins and kill the general. That's why he had spoken up. And because he'd opened his big mouth, he now lay on a stretcher, carried by four of Al Handy's hardcases. In light of Al Handy's past failures, Amos Wade had explained it, they had a better chance of success if one of them did the job. Hez knew himself not to be an overly brave man. His present location, inside a tightly secured fort, did little to reassure him. It

147

did serve to make his imposture more believable.

Gray army blanket tucked to his chin, he lay pale and trembling, beads of oily sweat covering his forehead. He looked every bit a man in shock with a severe injury. At the direction of the orderlies, Handy's men carried him into a treatment room near the "T" intersection of the hall that gave access to the three wards. Across the way was a private room—the one, he knew, where General Frank Corrington lay, still unconscious from last report. Once the stretcher came to rest on the floor, he steeled himself for what came next.

Sucking in a deep breath, he tightly gripped the big knife in his right hand and gave a nod to Handy's gunhawks. They struck swiftly, downing all three orderlies in the room with fatal knife wounds. One made a rasping, gurgling sound that set Manning's jangled nerves to shrieking.

"Okay, it's done," Frank Granger, in the sergeant's uniform, said roughly. "Time for you to get in there and fix the general, Mr. Manning."

Reluctantly, Hez Manning climbed off the stretcher and flexed his legs to stimulate circulation. He felt dizzy, his thoughts giddy. Through the open door, he saw the closed portal that separated him from his target. Gripping the knife even tighter, he advanced into the hall.

Three of the hardcases came with him. So far everything had gone according to plan, and confidence buoyed them. Then the door to Corrington's room flew open, and Eli Holten stepped out.

Eli Holten stood at the foot of Frank Corrington's bed. He had outlined to Frank everything he intended to accomplish with the present campaign. They had talked of what Eli had done in Arizona, of the Apaches and how they differed from the tribes of the high plains. Shyly, Eli had confided his strong, paternal feelings for

148

Sarah-Jane and Michael Clemmer and his regret that he had been unable to rescue Bobby Clemmer from the Comanches. At last they had talked themselves out, and Frank showed signs of fatigue.

His eyes drooped, and his head nodded when Eli rose at last and started for the door. Frank's voice, drifting somewhat, arrested Eli's motion.

"It's going to be a tough one, Eli."

A partial grin gave his mouth a lopsided angle. "Yep. And I sure miss the cigars and brandy."

"You know where they are," Frank forced out. "That is if the brigade sergeant major hasn't helped himself a little too liberally."

"Quinn deserves them. He's a good man. We'll get those outlaws for you, Frank. Every damned one."

At the door Eli paused again. "Good night, Frank."

Holten turned to find himself facing Manning and four armed men. The Remington filled his hand without conscious effort. The blast of the detonating cartridge in the severely confined space drowned out a shouted alarm.

"For Christ's sake it's Holten!"

Eli's first bullet took a knife-wielding hardcase in the chest. The edged weapon clattered loudly on the polished wooden floor as the outlaw let it go and staggered backward. Holten ignored him to fire at the nearest threat. His .44 barked again, and the man sat down, an expression of puzzlement on his face. Abruptly he began to weep like a lost child. Holten had no time for that, either. Behind the last man he shot, he recognized the bulky figure of Hez Manning.

Eyes sunken into dark pits gave Manning a skull-like appearance, enhanced by hollow cheeks. His rusty blond hair and thick brows were accentuated by his ghostly pallor. He, too, carried a knife, and he raised it now to strike at Eli Holten. Close at hand, Eli heard the alarm in raised voices. Army boot heels pounded along the hall. It seemed like slow motion as Hez Manning

149

lunged toward him.

"Corporal of the Guard, trouble in the dispensary. Turn out the guard," the chief hospitaler brayed from the small front porch.

Manning still came at him, the mouth under those hate-glowing eyes twisted into an ugly shout of rage. *Take him alive,* Holten goaded himself. The knife cut flat and level through space where Eli's belly had been a moment before. He took still another backstep, angling toward the corner of the hall. Manning came after him.

His attacker might be swimming in molasses, Holten gauged, from the maddening slowness with which everything seemed to happen. Manning raised the knife and struck downward. The tip caught in the leather of Holten's vest and sliced through, removing the entire left side. That could have been his heart, Holten realized with a twinge of unease. Manning lunged again, arm extended like a fencer.

"Well, shit," Holten said softly with resignation as he triggered a round that struck Manning in the left nostril.

Eli's bullet scrambled a third of Manning's brain and blew off the back of his head before it exited and struck the wall. Three armed men, their Springfields at the ready, thundered down the hall. Holten looked at the lead man and deliberately aimed for his thigh. Not wanting any more of this fight, the man turned and ran.

Glass shattered in the single window of the room in which the other two hardcases had ducked for cover. They bailed out a moment before Eli Holten shot the escaping outlaw in the shoulder, who in turn stumbled and disappeared around the corner into the ward hall. Holten started after him when the breaking glass registered on him. More of them.

Holten burst into the room in time to see the hardcases swing their legs over the sill and drop into the darkness beyond. Eli fired a useless shot, answered at

150

once by three rifles out on the parade ground. Horses' hooves pounded the sun-baked parade, and shouts rose from the confused guards and a furious sergeant of the guard.

Surprisingly the fleeing outlaws headed for the stables instead of the main gate. Lost among the confined horses and mules, a jumble of buildings preventing a clear line of sight, they hastily steered their stolen mounts to the low, narrow gate in the low wall. There they dismounted and led the animals to safety on the far side.

Quickly they disappeared in the cluster of hovels that had grown up outside the fort. Cursing foully, the Sergeant of the Guard called off his men. Before a proper search could be organized, the escaped assassins would be well mounted on fresh horses and miles away. Holten reported back to Frank Corrington.

"I'm going to insist on an armed guard at your door, and that door locked until we make an end of all this. One of our trio of conspirators is dead. I shot him outside here. Damn, how I wanted to question him."

"It happened too fast, Eli," Corrington said gently. "No blame attaches to you. Now get out of here, get some sleep and go after the rest."

His crooked, most boyish smile in place, Eli Holten drew himself up and saluted his old friend. "Good as done, General."

"We got rights, mister. You can't make us leave."

"You'll leave on your own," Lieutenant Robert Fuller informed the prospector, "or you'll leave in chains, to face a military tribunal. You are illegally on ceded treaty land. You have one hour."

"Why, we can hardly pack half our outfit in that time," the bearded gold-seeker protested.

"Then leave it."

The 12th U.S. Cavalry had come to the Black Hills.

Flanking companies had located several Sioux and Cheyenne war parties during their sweep. Corporal Newcomb's Crow scouts had made contact and informed the leaders that the army wanted them back on the reservations. Neither the Sioux nor Cheyenne liked the Crow, but they respected them. They accepted it as true that the army had not come to punish them. Still they had grievances they wanted aired. Lt. Larry Beekman, who accompanied the Crow scouts, suggested a parlay. Each war band agreed to meet at Place of Rocks on the Inyan Kara River. Swift patrols of platoon strength went beyond the Hills, accompanied by the Crow scouts, to locate other warrior bands believed headed toward the disputed land. By the time the main detachment reached the Black Hills, word came also of someone else found on the prairie.

In camp, late the afternoon after routing the last gang of prospectors, Eli Holten waited with considerable trepidation for the arrival of the Thorne sisters. He could hardly believe it. What in hell had Gabe Thorne got in his mind to allow five young white women to wander the prairie in the middle of a buildup to a general uprising? The old man must have gone senile, Ei concluded. When word passed at last of riders coming in, Eli stood in the middle of the camp, fists on hips.

"Eli! Oh, Eli, I just knew we'd find you!" Melissa squealed as she recognized the tall, lean, buckskin-clad figure standing in a posture of suppressed anger.

"What are you doing out here?" he thundered, holding her away from him as she tried to twine her arms around his neck.

"Why, we came to find you. Paw's ailing, the boys are off with the cows, and we're short on every sort of supply. We needed help."

"We need something else, too," Doreen boldly advised him, her eyes fixed on his crotch.

"Now don't you start that, young la—" Eli started,

152

only to be engulfed by Samantha, Susanna and Helen.

"Some fellers have all the luck," a burly line sergeant observed.

Holten's scowl silenced him, but not the flurry of guffaws that ran among the troops. Carefully extricating himself from the arms, soft breasts, legs and torsos, he at last stood apart. The enormity of the danger they were in still plagued him.

"Don't you realize you could have been killed? The tribes are talking about an uprising."

Doreen and the twins managed to look sheepish. "We didn' know anything about that," Doreen informed him, low and throatily.

"Didn't you see any Indians?" Holten probed.

"Oh, sure. We ran into the nicest Cheyenne fellers. Boy named Spotted Hawk. He said to tell you hello. He an' his friends rode with us to near the Belle Fourche River."

"My God," Holten blurted. "Spotted Hawk's leading one of the larger war parties."

"He saw my necklace," Melissa put in. "The one you sent me for Christmas a couple of years back."

Holten recalled it in a rush. It had been worked in a bead pattern that also rendered it a safe conduct. If the Cheyenne honored it, perhaps there might be a way to end all of this without a bloody Indian war. The knowledge gave Eli the first good news since Frank Corrington had regained consciousness.

"Now that we're here, when can we go to Fort Rawlins?" Susanna asked.

"Not . . . for a long time, I'm afraid. We're on a difficult campaign and can't spare anyone to escort you, which means you come along."

"Oh, wonderful," Helen enthused, clapping her hands.

"Not so wonderful," Holten corrected. "It'll be rough, dangerous, and utterly boring."

"Oh, no, not at all boring," Doreen modified, again

sizing up the ample bulge of Holten's at-rest member.

"Doreen, we're in the middle of an army bivouac."

"That's no problem. You'd be surprised how we can manage a quiet, private place."

"I'm sure I would be. But it's . . . out . . . of the . . . question."

Giggling, Samantha and Susanna rushed to hug Eli's arms. "Wait until tonight and say that, Eli," Samantha whispered in his ear.

Holten had barely gotten to sleep, the military encampment finally quieted and at rest, when he sensed the presence of someone close by. Before he could rouse enough to open an eye and look around, he felt the soft, silken slide of bare flesh along his back, under the covers. A suppressed giggle and sweet, warm breath caressed his ear.

"It's me, Eli, Samantha."

"Now, dammit, I—"

More warm, pliable flesh slithered down his chest and abdomen, and a strong, lithe leg hooked over his. He gasped involuntarily when a small, moist hand grasped his semi-erect phallus. A tongue began to lap at his right nipple.

"I brought Helen along. She's feelin' left out. 'Lissa an' the rest have made a nice little nest for us, out beyond the horse line, but I thought we'd have a little extra fun first."

"Samantha," Holten whispered harshly, then gasped again as Helen began to rub the sensitive tip of his rapidly increasing organ in her hot, wet, ever so ready cleft. "How can you . . . how can I, . . . Oooh, hell, how can anyone say no at a time like this?"

"That's the spirit," Helen chirped as she guided him to a rich, tight reward.

Abandoning his defensive mein, along with his reservations, Eli plunged deeply within the barely yielding furnace of Helen's desires. Once past that obstacle, he gave himself freely and with ardor, knowing full well there would be more, a whole lot more, all night long.

Mason Ashford stood outside the splendid front of the Prairie House Hotel in Pierre. He considered the place pretentious. Why ever had Amos Wade decided to move here? No matter. He had an important message to deliver from Governor Stratton. It might as well be a suite here as Wade's former residence. He entered with all his huffy hauteur intact. The slight, delicate-featured room clerk took him in at a glance and added special warmth to a beaming smile of welcome. Here was one of his own.

"May I help you?"

"Mr. Amos Wade's room, please?" Ashford lisped. Now why did he feel so distinctly uncomfortable around this—this menial?

"Suite Four-ten, top floor,"

"Thank you." Ashford iclly sent his message of rejection.

"Should I whistle up the speaking tube and announce you?"

"Oh, heavens no. You needn't blow . . . on that thing on my account."

"I don't mind." The clerk batted his eyelashes. "I'm used to it."

Ashford took the first flight of stairs, to the landing, two at a time. He roughly took hold of himself and settled his flustered emotions. With considerably more decorum, he continued to the fourth floor. A soft knock on the center door of the suite and he found himself face to face with Al Handy.

"Ah—er, M-Mr. Wade, please."

"C'mon in, runt," Handy growled. He still stung from the loss of good men.

155

"What is it, Ashford? The governor have a wild hair up his ass?"

"One might say that, if one was addicted to the vulgar," Ashford answered prissily.

"Stop being the arbiter of social intercourse and get to the point," Zack Walters snarled.

Clearing his throat, Ashford began in a higher register than he had intended. "Governor Stratton and I are extremely disturbed about one of our key men, one of the principals for God's sake, being gunned down by Eli Holten. We were unaware Holten had returned to the territory."

"Well, you know now," Amos Wade responded. "And I imagine it disturbed poor Hez Manning a whole hell of a lot more than it did the governor."

"Yes, I suppose so. All the same, the governor has impressed upon me the importance of securing from you gentlemen a solemn promise that in the future you will pay less attention to getting personal vengeance on Eli Holten and Frank Corrington and put more effort into pressuring the Indians into open warfare."

His face thunderous, Amos Wade nearly exploded. When he calmed enough to speak in a nearly normal tone, his words were clipped as though someone strangled him. "We will do exactly that. In fact that is what this meeting you interrupted was about. We are preparing to start something else, something monumental enough to assure the savages will attack with unbounded ferocity."

"And when is this to occur?"

"Within the next two or three days, Ashford."

"What might I tell the governor to be looking for?"

Amos Wade gave him a sardonic smile. "How about an attack on a reservation?"

CHAPTER 15

"There's a good job well done," Lt. Robert Fuller remarked as he stood with Eli Holten, watching the Sioux and Cheyenne trail off from Place of Rocks on Inyan Kara Creek.

"Don't be too quick to celebrate, Bob," Eli Holten answered.

"Why not? They agreed to go back to their villages, didn't they?"

Holten shook his head. "Spotted Hawk didn't. He and White Horse had their village completely wiped out. Together they command over forty warriors. And they're not leaving the Black Hills country until they're satisfied with how the white killers are punished."

"We're taking care of that," Fuller declared.

"So far we've not run into any of Al Handy's men, or the ones behind all this. What we don't need is to have some forty or fifty Cheyennes painted for war following along near us. We also have an important visit to make."

"Where?"

"Pine Ridge. Those promises to go back to the agencies are good only so long as the whites do no more harm. There may be a problem with Spotted Hawk. There sure as hell can be one with the Sioux. They are closer to the Black Hills, and there are more of them.

I've already cleared it with Mayberry. We take a detachment of a reinforced platoon and ride now."

Two ridges separated them from the main column now. Already, Helen and the twins had second thoughts about their precipitous departure, especially in defiance of Eli Holten's specific orders to remain while he visited the Sioux Agency at Pine Ridge. They had left the wagon behind, but Melissa told them confidently that there would be enough fresh, green graze for the horses and the single pack animal they led would carry enough food for them. It still didn't silence all opposition.

Helen reined in her dapple-gray and called ahead to her eldest sister. "Why are we doin' this?"

Melissa and the others halted. Melissa turned back with an expression of disgust twisting her face. "Enough of that, little sister. We've been over it and over it, and we decided."

"*You* decided, 'Lissa," Helen accused. "I still want to know why."

Melissa snorted with impatience. "Because Eli's not payin' us any attention, that's why. We were like orphans dragging along with the army. We have to *show* him."

Only half convinced, Doreen added her support. "Sure. When Eli comes back and finds us gone, he'll remember all right. An' he'll be sorry. He'll come after us, and we'll be happy ever after."

"I—I'm not so sure," Helen replied, worry plain on her face. "He'll be mad as blazes we didn't do what he said."

"Oh, pooh. Eli's a man, silly. A clever woman can lead him around by his dingus."

Helen's face looked like she wanted to cry. "I don't feel very clever right now."

158

"Me neither," muttered Susanna. "Nor me," Samantha complained.

"That's enough of that," Melissa steamed. "I'm oldest, and you'll do as I say. The Indians have given up. We've got nothing to be afraid of. Three days and we'll be at Fort Rawlins, waiting for Eli to return."

Eli Holten and Lieutenant Robert Fuller arrived with their detachment in the largest Sioux encampment on the Pine River Agency during mid-afternoon. The eyanpaha rode ahead of them through the rings of lodges, bearing aloft his feather-decorated staff of office and calling out the visitors' identities. His spotted, gray and blue-black horse cavorted in tight little circles at each knot of curious who turned out to see this unusual event.

"Mahto Tanka of the Oglalahca comes. Make way for Tall Bear!" he cried out. "Our old friend, the Blue Coat Soldier Chief, Pahaha Fuller comes."

Later, after the quiet, solemn greetings had been exchanged with White Bull of the Sans Arcs and Lame Bear of the Hunkpapa, the camp crier went his rounds again, announcing a feast with dancing and drumming that night, and a council for the next day. Holten and Fuller were given a lodge to make their own, while arrangements for the detachment to erect their tents on the edge of the village set the soldiers to work.

"Well, Curly Head Fuller," Holten began with a chuckle while he unpacked his saddlebags and laid out his bead- and quill-decorated Sioux shirt, trousers and moccasins. "It appears you've acquired some new stature with the Sioux since I last saw you."

"Don't laugh," Robert Fuller retorted. "I take it quite seriously."

"Which you should. If they thought you didn't, you'd have a hell of a time getting any cooperation

159

from then on."

"And you, Tall Bear? I see you're going to dress the part."

"Habit," Holten explained. "It also gives me an advantage no strictly white man will ever enjoy. If I dress and talk like an equal, they'll treat me as one." He gave Fuller a shrewd wink. "It also gives us one more vote on the council."

Fuller produced a droll expression. "And you're the one who complains about civilization and politicians."

"You don't think it will work? Hide and watch and see what happens."

The feast went well. Lame Bear and White Bull apologized repeatedly for not having buffalo to strengthen their friends' bodies. They made much of having only antelope, venison and issue beef, which they called "stinking meat." Wisely, from past experience with Curly Head Fuller, they refrained from mentioning that the tasty third course, a rich, brown stew, was made of fresh, plump puppy dog. The drumming began before the last course of boiled, sweetened cattail root had been served.

Lieutenant Fuller found both feet moving to the rhythm of the drums. His body picked up the beat. "It sort of gets to you," he observed, licking his fingers.

Eli Holten studied Bob Fuller's obsidian eyes, high cheekbones and noble arch of nose with amusement. "They say that a person can't be reached by the music unless he has Indian blood. To a true white, it is only a lot of noisy beating of drums."

Puzzled and off balance, Fuller queried, "What brought on that observation?"

"What does he say?" White Bull inquired.

"*Pahaha* is discovering that he is not entirely *wásicun,*" Holten replied with a chuckle.

Both old chiefs nodded wisely. "We wondered how

long it would take him," Lame Bear stated drolly.

After the ritual welcome dance, two "fancy" dances, and a spirit dance to insure blessings on the council, the all male dancers withdrew, and a slow, syncopated beat came from the drums. The social dances had begun. The women and girls, in a variety of dresses of animal skins and white-made cloth, danced into the performing area and formed a large circle. After two circuits, they began to dance out as individuals and select a man from the assembled feasters. Redwing, a lovely, young Sans Arc widow, twitched her lips invitingly and swayed to the music as she gestured for Lieutenant Robert Fuller to join her.

Grinning boyishly, Fuller rose and went to her side. Hands clasped, with their arms crossed over at the wrists, they began the simple two-step dance as they advanced toward the circle. Long tassles of her bead- and quill-decorated shawl swaying in rhythm, Redwing was a vision of beauty and grace. Eli Holten looked on with amused interest.

His appreciation of the situation increased when Redwing held on to Fuller for a second dance, then a third. After the fourth, a more energetic, intricate dance, Fuller and Redwing disappeared. Holten had little doubt as to where.

"This is your lodge?" Fuller asked. His past two years attempting to master the Lakota tongue had paid off enough to let him converse with at least the facility of a ten-year-old.

"Come in, come in," Redwing urged him. The hot glow in her eyes left no doubt for Lieutenant Fuller as to where this home visit would lead.

Inside, Redwing removed her shawl and moccasins. Then she turned and closed the entrance flap. That would insure privacy. She swayed when she walked, as though still dancing. Temptingly she closed the distance between them. Nimble fingers, accustomed to working with porcupine quills, unfastened the buttons

161

of Bob Fuller's tunic. Then came his shirt.

His breathing grew rough as she peeled him out of the long-sleeve, dark-blue wool. He sat down abruptly and tugged on his boots. Redwing smiled and nodded. While he struggled with his second boot, she raised the hem of her elkhide dress and pulled it over her head. Underneath she wore a sort of diaperlike garment. Fuller reached out and spanned her narrow waist with his big, hard hands.

Redwing tittered shyly and guided his fingers to the tie points, so that he released her underwear. The soft, amazingly thin piece of pliable doeskin dropped to the cured-hide floor liner. Bob Fuller gaped at her youthful, flawless beauty. He rose and embraced her, drawing her against the rigid, upthrust proof of his interest.

Soon he was free of all encumbrances. Their naked bodies writhed against each other as they embraced. Bob tasted deeply of her mouth, while she ran eager hands up and down his firm, muscular back. Redwing raised one leg and began to slide the inside surface of it against the outside of his. Slowly he lowered her to a thick nest of buffalo robes. Redwing lay back luxuriantly, spread wide her legs and let one delicate hand stray to the edge of her hairless cleft.

Idly her fingers spread the lips. A flower of great delight bloomed before Bob's eager eyes. He went to his knees, his member rigid and aching from the intensity of his arousal. With studied tenderness, hastened by overwhelming ardor, he brought the link that would join them into thrilling contact with heated, coppery flesh. The pink portals widened, welcoming him.

"Red—wing . . . aaaah, Redwing," he murmured softly as he thrust his pulsing manhood into her hot, yielding softness.

Shortly before the final dance ended, Sergeant Malloy came to where Eli Holten sat with the chiefs.

"I've come to report the bivouac secure for the night, sir. Where's Lieutenant Fuller?"

Unable to restrain himself, Holten answered with a big, happy smile. "Right now, Sergeant Malloy, I suspect the Lieutenant is in the pleasant process of getting his brains screwed out."

Wearing a beautiful, intricately made feather mantle, Chief White Bull opened the council. Lieutenant Fuller sat with droopy eyes, evidence that he had spent little of the night in sleep. Holten had greeted him with a smirk, but asked no questions and offered no comment. The older and wiser heads among the council spoke for peace. It was not often the soldiers would fight to protect the Sioux. Why not let them? After the ritual pipe had gone its rounds and individual speakers had their opportunities, Holten took the pipe and stood to speak.

"Only harm to your families can come from leaving the reservation to fight against the whites who break the treaty and their own laws. Even as we speak," he told the blank-face audience, "the pony soldiers and the walking soldiers are searching out those who do wrong. They will be punished. In these days, keeping the peace with honor is more important than trying to regain it from the fury of battle. Those who have suffered, even those who have gone to the Spirit World, will be avenged."

"No!" one of the hot-headed young men blurted, his fingers not yet tightly closed on the pipe. "White Bull said a true thing earlier, only he twisted the words. The white soldiers have *never* done anything to help the Sioux. Tall Bear is wise, and brave, but he, too, asks the wrong questions. Why should we believe them now? Why would the soldiers side with us, against their own kind?"

Sentiment swayed one way, then the other, as the

163

gathered chiefs and the audience expressed their positions. At last Holten took the pipe a second time. "You know me. Those who do not, have heard about me. When I was the age of Many Ponies"—Holten gestured with his chin in proper Sioux manners—"I thought of nothing but the glory of fighting, of counting coup. I was proud. I was an Oglala warrior. Now I live as my white side dictates. It is not always easy. It rarely brings me glory. Every time I return to my adopted people, I become a different man. I know again the clean life, the clear path to honor and the sweet freedom of living like a true man. The thrill of the hunt means more than the praise of white men. Warm, clean rain in my face washes my body better than all the flower smells of white man's soap. The laughter of children, the delicious aroma of food cooking out of doors, the haunting whistle of wind through the lodge poles at the top of the tipi, sweet grass and blue sky, the thrill engendered by the *Eyanpaha*'s shrill cry—all of these things call to me. I do not lie. I do not speak with two tongues, one for the Sioux and one for the white man. I would rather face torture and die than to be false to my chosen people.

"I came because it is true. Beside me sits a soldier chief. He speaks for General Corrington, Bull Elk, as you name him. You know he is a man of honor. Bull Elk says the soldiers do not come to fight the Sioux or the Cheyenne. We are here to drive the whites off your sacred lands. Give us the chance to do that. Stay in your lodges. Do not fight unless you are attacked. I see you with eyes of love. I see you with pride. Make all men see you as I do. I have spoken."

White Bull rose. "Tall Bear has spoken well. He gives much to think about. We will go each to his own lodge and think on this. We will eat and sleep and meet again when the sun returns."

A single drum stroke ended the council. Holten

walked away toward the cavalry camp with Lieutenant Fuller.

"I gather we didn't win a hell of a lot," Fuller said in disappointment.

"We didn't lose, either," Holten reminded him.

Eighty miles due east of the big council meeting, on the Rosebud Reservation, Al Handy waited at the head of a blood-hungry body of sixty-five men. His surviving twenty-seven followers had been augmented by thirty-eight prospectors, miners, drifters and general frontier population—anyone, in fact, who wanted to "take a shot at a couple of greasy Injuns." Their target, a sleeping Yankton village removed by some thirty miles from the Agency center, waited for them in the valley ahead.

Spread over a long, winding meadow, individual clans and warrior societies formed into separate hoops of lodges, the Yankton village extended some two and a quarter miles with a span of nearly three-quarters of a mile. Smoke from banked fires drifted lazily from the open tops of many lodges. Some traditional dwellings had been replaced with government issue canvas; other families had opted for brush and log hovels, more in a style blended of Navajo hogans and white men's wilderness cabins. Among the favored war ponies tethered by tradition outside lodges, several wagons showed prominently. Compelled to live within strictly defined limits, with little room to rove as in the past, the old ways were dying, to be replaced with a new way that was neither Indian nor white.

Such subtleties made no impression on the hardcases and Indian haters waiting to rush down on the undefended inhabitants of the Yankton village. They sat and smoked in the thick pine and juniper forest along the ridge and passed bottles of whiskey among their fellow marauders. Mercy, forgiveness, or even loyalty were qualities entirely foreign to their natures. They had made their credo to get it over the other guy. To use violence as the first, rather than a last, resort, they accepted as the norm. The majority, including Handy's outlaws, would sell their mothers for even a modest profit. The Indians below, unaware and unprepared, would receive far less consideration.

"We'd better be goin'," Lane Parker, Al Handy's second in command, suggested.

"Right, Lane. You got tight enough rein on those drunken scum over there?"

"Sure. It's just Dutch courage, Al. Townies out to shoot themselves an Injun so's to have something to brag about to their grandkids. First arrow that zips past their ears, they'll sober up. Only hope they don't run like jackrabbits."

"You'd better. Our lives depend on it. There's maybe fifty warriors in that band. Could get kind of rough. Surprise is our best ally. Now, let's do it."

CHAPTER 16

Eyes cloaked in night watched the outlaws making ready, and had marked their position and strength. Long before the white marauders moved into line to attack the sleeping village, lean, grim-faced men led their best running ponies out of the herd and sped off in search of help. They went to other bands on their own reservation and some to distant Pine Ridge. Not surprisingly, a messenger had not been sent to the Agency office or the Indian Police. The Yanktonai had little faith in getting help from that source. The moon had waxed full and, although rising late, aided their desperate race for reinforcements.

It also benefited the whites gathered on the ridge. When the fat, waxy globe rose through a quarter of the sky, Al Handy gave the signal for the advance. At a walk initially, the sixty-five Indian haters worked their way clear of the trees. Once in the open, the pace increased to trot. Six men swung away to deal with the boys guarding the horse herd. The main force grew restless with anticipation and gladly spurred their mounts to a quick canter.

Nearing the darkened lodges, the horses stretched into a gallop. A rifle spat flame into the night, then two more, half a dozen. All along the line, weapons roared and flame lanced toward the helpless village. Then a line of warriors raised out of the screening brush and fired their weapons. Hot lead and moaning arrows met the on-coming white men. At once the Yanktonai braves ducked down again. Answering fire lashed nothing but air.

Again the warriors rose and fired a ragged volley. Horses screamed and stumbled; men cursed or cried in agony. Driven by their hatred of redmen, they again ventilated nothing. A third time the Yanktonai blazed away, ducked out of sight and, this time, moved to new locations on the right flank. The attackers' line had become a convex arc, like a bent bow. When the braves fired again, more of the attackers shrieked in pain. They reached the outer lodges, only to meet more resistance. War clubs whirred through the air, and lances stabbed with deadly accuracy. Whistles began to blow, and men took up their leader's desperate yell.

"Back. Turn back. Regroup at the trees."

Punishing fire followed them. Three hours remained until sunrise. How many hours until they got relief? The question tormented the Yankton chief who had haughtily disdained attending the unusual council at Pine Ridge.

Young men, jealous of their elders' symbols of authority, strutted in their most elaborate headdresses, and wore eagle-bone breast plates, ornate bracelets, arm bands and all the scalp locks they possessed. Feathers fluttered like a congregation of peacocks. They kept up a constant stir, pacing back and forth beyond where the interested men of several villages squatted to listen to the council at the center of the commotion.

White Bull had been speaking for some time, urging the people to accept the army's way, one that promised to them at least the hope of peace. Innate courtesy, forged since earliest childhood, prevented any of the younger, more intemperate men from hooting or jeering. Many of them made it plain by their expressions that they would have liked to. Principal among them was Many Ponies, who strutted the most insolently, each stomp of a moccasin raising dust in a plume around his rigid leg. Several of his companions in dissent blew incessantly on eagle wing-bone whistles, high, shrill, discordant notes.

"When they were children, we laughed at their moods," Iron Blanket spoke when the pipe passed to him. "They are no longer children."

"This is so," Yellow Horse of the Oglala agreed, scowling at Many Ponies and the antics of the young men. "Would you have the *akicita* scatter them as they would other rude persons?"

"The camp police. A serious alternative," White Bull injected. "We came to decide if we will keep the peace and let the blue coats do their work. Such childish doings should not deflect us from our deliberations. Besides, Many Ponies and three others of those acting foolishly are members of this council, with voting sticks of their own to cast."

"Then let's say what is on everyone's mind," Raven declared. "Do we let the young men take up the pipe of war? Or do we keep the peace, live as the whites wish us and let the soldiers avenge the wrongs to our sacred lands?"

"The vote!" Iron Blanket shouted.

Even as White Bull bent to retrieve the council pipe, the *Eyanpaha* trotted rapidly through the hoops of lodges, shouting clear and high, leading an exhausted young brave on a lathered, winded pony.

"White man trouble comes to our brothers the Yanktonai! Here comes a messenger with black news. More than five two-hands of white killers attack the village of Crow Fighter on the Rosebud Agency. Make way!"

His news electrified the council. Murmurs of

consternation rippled through the assembly. The younger men began to yip and do impromptu dance steps, celebrating the taking of the war path.

"Come, brothers. While the white devils kill our brothers the Yanktonai, we will find their homes and families, burn, kill, scalp, degrade their women," Many Ponies shouted.

Many agreed, even some of the older chiefs. "The closest ones will do. All whites are alike," Bent Rib shouted.

"No," Eli Holten bellowed. "No, listen to me. Their women and children do not make war on you. Why attack the helpless? We will all ride to the Rosebud and strike at the real enemy."

Singly and in groups of three and four the young men shouted him down. Seeking a shocker that would return them to reason, Holten looked about him with mounting worry. What could he do? Sioux women and children would be dying at the Yankton village, so white women and children should die in retaliation, thus reasoned the youthful warriors. So far they only made noise. Not one of them had seized the war pipe. *The war pipe!* Inspiration filled him with direction.

"Oṅśimaya! Oṅśimaya!" Holten shouted, raising the war pipe and commanding recognition. *"Oyate nimkte wacin yelo!* I want the people to live," he repeated himself. "I take the pipe of war against the white enemy at the Rosebud! Who follows the pipe? *Tuwe zuya, tuwe zuya?"*

"What the hell? I couldn't catch all of that," Lieutenant Fuller asked as the young men of the Pine Ridge Agency and those visiting for the council exploded into shouts of their prowess, vying to win honored places close to this Oglala war leader, Tall Bear.

"I took up the war pipe before any of these hotheads could. I told them I would fight so that they could live. They'll follow us to the Rosebud."

"I got that last. You asked who was going to war."

"Right," Holten said tight-lipped.

"Well, I know for sure I am."

"I've got blisters on my butt."

"I doubt that, Helen," Melissa stated in a bored tone.

"I want to go back."

"We can't do that, little sister."

"'Lissa, this is wrong. We shoulda stayed with the army, like Eli said to," Helen expounded, her appeal reduced by frustration to a whine.

Patiently, Melissa tried a new tack. "You're a grown woman now, Helen. You're goin' on fifteen. I know it's taking longer than we expected. Maybe we wandered too far north of where we should be."

"Maybe? I know for one thing that we ain't on the high road. There ain't any wagon tracks, and there ain't any wagons."

Melissa scanned the wide, empty prairie, then studiously examined the toes of her boots, unwilling to meet her sister's eyes. "I, ah, took a short-cut. I thought it would save time. We must have gotten turned around. I'm sorry, Helen. I'm sorry, Sam, Susie, Reenie," she ended in a squeak as tears flooded away any more words.

Doreen, always the practical one, took charge. "Don't you worry, 'Liss. It'll all work out. If we're too far north, we go south awhile. And tonight, I'll shoot us some rabbits for supper. How's that?"

"Oooh, Reenie," Melissa sobbed, relieved to be free of decision making for even one short afternoon.

Their new course took them sharply south of the line they had followed. Intent on finding the wide, well-traveled westward trail, the Thorn sisters missed the main course at a river ford, when the stout current carried them far down stream in the rapid spring rain runoff. Shortly before evening they made camp some ten miles south of the trail, only a scant distance from the northern boundary of the Rosebud Agency.

Unexpected and highly efficient resistance kept the fighting going at the Yankton encampment. Daylight found the opposing forces engaged in charge and counter-attack maneuvers that flared intermittantly all through the morning and into the afternoon. Al Handy pulled back his forces at three o'clock, under an uncomfortably warm sun. Sporadic sniping continued as individual warriors, or two-man teams foraged out to fire into the trees from a network of gullies that fed the creek.

"Those red niggers know something we didn't know they knew," Handy opened his strategy meeting.

"What the hell does that jumble o' words mean?" Bret Holly asked.

"They're fightin' like white men, like soldiers," Handy explained his torturous grammar.

Among the first to go onto the reservations, the Yanktonai had contributed volunteers to the army to serve as Indian scouts over the past several years. Many of those young men had been returning to the only home they knew, the agency. They had not been employed against their brothers, or the Cheyenne, rather the army—in an uncharacteristic burst of good sense—had assigned them to scout during the Ute uprising, and against the Comanches and Kiowas. Young, curious, and highly intelligent, the Yanktonai learned by observing as well as doing. They brought those talents home with them.

Their tactics kept the outlaw band pinned down, unable to launch another major assault, or to withdraw. Deeply ingrained distrust of the BIA's Indian agents, the Indian Police—usually made up of the toadies, the lazy, and the discontent—and the

172

green, untrained troops stationed on the reservations prevented seeking the closest source of reinforcements. In spite of that, the messengers sent for help produced results. Before noon warriors from camps close at hand began to arrive, in groups of twos and threes. Most of them reached Crow Fighter's village without being seen by the enemy.

Which resulted in Al Handy making a woefully inaccurate estimate of the situation. He didn't have the slightest idea of the numbers his sixty-man force faced. Five had died and several were wounded, which left him with approximately even odds, instead of outnumbering the Yanktonai by two to one as he had done at the outset. He knew nothing of the reinforcements, or of those yet on the way. Worse, he had observed but didn't give sufficient weight to the fact that the Indian forces were being directed by sharp young men with recent military combat experience.

"We can't stay here for long," he went on briefing his subordinates. "I'd say no longer than noon tomorrow."

"What's our chances of just pullin' out?" Bret Holly queried.

Handy frowned. "Not too good. We'd take losses for nothing. They, ah, they got some bucks in place behind us. Once we started to move, they'd hit us from both sides. The answer is a fast moving attack that'll carry us inside the village. When those lodges start burning, they'll lose it. They'll forget all about this tricky way of fighting and come at us any which way, like Injuns usually fight. Ever' man will want to protect his own, and to hell with holding a line."

"When do we do it?" Lamar Owens asked.

"Soon. I'd say a little after sundown," Handy informed him. "Now, here's the way we'll split up, so's we can hit from three directions at once. That's how Chivington did it at Sand Creek, an' Custer at the Washita. Injuns can't handle that sort of thing. Too bad we don't have a band; that drives 'em nuts. So, Lamar, you'll take twenty men an' go to the north. The rest of you . . ."

Riding the warm waves of a spring day, the orange-tinged ball of the sun had a good hour before plunging over the curve of the earth. The Sioux warriors from Pine Ridge, along with Eli Holten and a platoon of the 12th U.S. Cavalry, had ridden hard all day, alternately walking and trotting. They came in from the west, which put them at the backs of Al Handy's outlaws. Scouts, all of them Sioux, reported back hastily.

Many white men, perhaps six two-hands of them, made ready to attack a Yanktonai village. They described the two oblique wings on the flanks of the main force, noting positions of long-range rifles and which men carried shotguns. Eager for battle, the younger Hunkpapa, Oglala and Sans Arc braves hooted and yelped their enthusiasm. They listened, though, when the older men, chosen as war chiefs because of their experience, gave them the plan of attack as outlined by Tall Bear Holten.

When all agreed, by silence more often than spoken acceptance, the large force deployed, with fifty Sioux warriors and the cavalry platoon in the center. By then, less than half a mile separated them from the battlefield. Holten smiled and nodded to Lieutenant Fuller.

"Over that second ridge, I would say," he informed the young officer.

Fuller nodded and continued in silence. To burden his men with the extra effort of holding carbines or revolvers at the ready during the closing action seemed excessive. When the large force neared the base of the second swale, he spoke quietly to the platoon sergeant.

"Sergeant, pass the word to draw carbines."

"Yes, sir."

To left and right the designated bands of warriors split off to circle north and south and sweep down on the rear of the unsuspecting outlaws. Half an hour of daylight remained. The twilight would linger for nearly an hour more. Time enough, Eli considered, to get the job done. The horses began to grunt and snort as they leaned into the slope they had to climb. A dozen feet from the crest, Lieutenant Fuller leaned forward, easing himself.

"Make ready," he snapped in a whisper.

"Sir!" Sergeant Rupp hissed.

Up to the top and over the rise. The enemy could be clearly seen below, eyes fixed on the village, with not a thought for what might lie behind. In ignorance of the powerful force at their backs, they began to deploy for the planned night attack. Once more, Lieutenant Fuller issued a terse order.

"Forward at the trot, Sergeant." A moment later, he added, "Gallop, hooo!"

Spread out now, the ranks of troopers and warriors sped toward the unsuspecting enemy. Smiling at the novelty of what the next command would do, Fuller raised his voice to full volume.

"Trumpeter, sound the charge!"

Crisp and clear, bell-like in their vibrancy, the bugle notes bounded across the bowllike valley. Yelling wildly, the war whoops of the Sioux answered the summons to battle. Below them, startled faces turned to see the double line of blue uniforms, roan mounts surging in long, downhill lunges. Horrified, their eyes recorded the smooth sweep of barrels as forty carbines came to shoulders. The keener ears among the outlaws heard over the thunder of hoofs the terrifying command, which the breeze caught and flung away.

"Commence . . . FIRE!"

In no time, the carefully planned assault on the Yanktonai village became a mass of desperate men, swirling and striking out in blind pandemonium as soldiers with clubbed rifles and barking revolvers, and warriors with lance, tomahawk and knife spilled over them like a rising tide. Three or four broke free, then a few more.

Before long a steady stream of frightened, disoriented riffraff and outlaw allies ran blindly from the horrors of their inglorious defeat. In the midst of the confusion, Eli Holten spotted Lamar Owens and edged Sonny close toward him. He wanted to capture Al Handy's chief lieutenant alive if possible. Owens saw and recognized Holten in the next confused second. He raised his hand, the muzzle of a smoking .44 Smith & Wesson American centering on Eli's face. Holten had no choice.

His Remington bucked in his hand, and he flung himself sideways a fraction of a second later. Lamar Owens' slug cut empty air and struck a Sioux warrior in his left shoulder. The outlaw lieutenant had less than a tenth of a second to enjoy even this Pyrrhic victory. Eli Holten's 230 grain .44 bullet took Lamar Owens in the hollow of his throat, pulping his larynx with hydrostatic shock and shattering two vertebrae as it exited the back of his neck. His spinal cord severed, he flopped onto the ground, a headless chicken in his final moments.

In full retreat now, Al Handy and his followers had no time to consider Lamar Owens' fate. They had only one idea in mind: head north. That way lay safety and a chance to regroup. By then the Indians and their soldier allies had joined forces in the welter of dead and wounded outlaws. Many of the younger ones streamed after the fleeing outlaws. Holten shouted for White Bull and the other chiefs to send the club men, the camp police, to turn them back.

"Don't let them leave the reservation," Holten urged. "They'll lose all the advantage we have now. This is our victory. Let the others go. We'll go after them, the army and I," he pleaded.

It took all the efforts of Holten, White Bull and the

other chiefs to prevent the blood-lusting young warriors from breaking the treaty by riding off the reservation. For Indians there was no such thing as a limit to "hot pursuit." Not until long after nightfall, nearing ten o'clock, did conditions return to normal in the Yanktonai village. Fires burned bright, drummers warmed up to play while exuberant warriors danced the victory. Despite the efforts of Holten and the soldiers, here and there could be seen a wetly red, circular patch of skin, with wisps of hair hanging prominently from one side. Now, with an even larger council, Eli argued once more to let the army find the wrongdoers and have them punished according to white man's law.

Flushed by the recent triumph, and proud of the selfless way the white soldiers had fought for the Sioux, the chiefs gave him overwhelming support. Pleased, grateful, and bone tired, Holten made ready to settle down for the night.

"Now, at least, we can go after these maggots without worrying about a full scale uprising," he said wearily to Lieutenant Fuller. "But that's for tomorrow. Tomorrow is good enough."

CHAPTER 17

Wide and low, a dark band of dirty gray hung over the western half of the sky. Tendrils ran eastward to the north and south of their course. Early morning on the Dakota plains offered little to lighten the mood of the survivors. They had ridden through most of the night, hiding out at last in a deep ravine until certain no one pursued them. Al Handy uttered muffled strings of curses from time to time. How had the army gotten involved? They were supposed to be kept out of it. The clouds piled higher, then grew blacker, as the badly battered outlaws worked their way north and west, toward the Black Hills. Handy estimated they had made some twenty-five miles off the reservation when the rain began to fall.

Good. It would wipe out any tracks. The warm spring shower grew heavier, and a brisk wind came up, plucking at their clothing. They had made another five mud-slogging miles when they came upon the remarkable travelers. Burt Sands, scouting out in front, located them first. He came trotting back to the drooping column of defeated men with a whoop and a wildly wicked expression.

"You won't believe what's found themselves a nice dry place out of the rain," he brayed to Al Handy.

"I'm in no mood for guessing games," Handy snarled.

Sands swallowed hard and blinked eyes wide and round with incredulity. "There's this abandoned soddy up the way about half a mile. I gave it a once-over, 'cause of the rain and all. An' who do you suppose beat me to it?"

"Dammit, Burt. Spit it out."

"It's girls, Al. Little-bitty white girls. Red hair and button noses, an' pretty as can be."

Twenty minutes later, Al Handy and his eighteen surviving hardcases crowded into the large central room of an abandoned soddy; those closest formed a circle around the Thorne sisters. Mutters of appreciation and hastily aroused lust rustled among the men. Wide-eyed and frightened, Melissa and Doreen confronted them on their feet. The twins and Helen huddled together before the hearth of a smokey fireplace.

"Wh-who are you?" Melissa demanded, hands whitely gripped around the stock of her Spencer repeater.

Right then the full fury of the storm broke outside. So close and powerful it actually lighted the interior of the old sod homestead, a bolt of lightning struck with a sizzle and instantaneous, rippling salvo of stupendous thunder. It left minds numb, eyes blank and motion frozen for two long, awesome seconds. Melissa shook herself, and a small moan escaped.

"Names don't matter all that much. How you all manage to be here?"

"We—ah—we're traveling to—to Fort Rawlins," Melissa blurted.

Handy rolled his eyes and smirked. "My, and there's five of you. Stand up, you three, let's get a look at you."

Helen complied, too frightened not to, while Samantha and Susanna refused. At a flick of Handy's thumb, two of his men stepped close to the twins and

179

yanked them to their feet.

"Prime meat if you ask me," one outlaw remarked, smacking his lips.

"Reckon they're able to service all of us'n?" a moon-faced hardcase asked of no one in particular.

"More than able, I'd say," another observed.

Al Handy clapped his hands together and rubbed them enthusiastically, like a man washing some stubborn stain from his skin. "Boys, it appears Providence has provided us with a good romp in the hay," he offered.

Now, the Thorn girls never minded a good romp in the hay. But pulling a train that long, without even the compensation of mutual affection, or at least a few dollars each, didn't sit well at all. Anger replaced fear in Melissa and Doreen. Small fist clinched, Melissa shook it under Al's nose.

"You can get that idea out of your head right now," she snapped. "There's only five of us, an'—an' . . ." She paused, counting. "Near to twenty of you. That's nigh on four of you apiece. No way we're gonna play pokey-holey with that many for less—for less than—two dollars, hard money, each."

"That's right," Doreen seconded, hands on breasts and pelvis jutted out to better display her many charms.

Handy laughed loud and sharply. "*You* are gonna charge *us?*"

"That's right, mister," Doreen answered, voice hard, eyes aglitter. "We've never sold it before; but times are hard, and we could use the money. Gen'rally we give it to boys and men we like. And, mister, we don't even know you, let alone like you."

His passion long suppressed, human urges being held back by days and weeks in the saddle, in dangerous fights and chases, Al Handy flamed. His phallus rose rigidly erect, straining against his trousers, aching for the soft, slippery touch that would give it release. With one big, hard hand he knocked the gun from her hand, then grabbed the top front of the mannish shirt worn by Melissa Thorne.

"How you figger to make us pay?" he taunted as he ripped downward, stripping buttons and laying bare her lovely, creamy textured breasts. He let go long enough to grab and yank at her belt, as lightning flashed and hail began to drum on the roof.

Melissa screamed, then quickly recovered herself. Her hand lashed out and solidly slapped Al Handy on the face. He began to laugh while with his free hand he groped at his crotch to free his raging manhood.

"Let her go! Damn you, let her go or we'll get Eli to fix you good," Doreen threatened.

"Eli?" Al Handy purred. "Who is Eli?"

"Eli Holten, that's who. He's an army scout and an Injun fighter, and the bravest, strongest man we know. And he's our friend. If you don't let us go, he'll hunt you down and put you in your grave."

"Oh—oh, my. I—I never realized," Al Handy mocked them. "You're friends of Eli Holten? Hey, boys, we got some of Eli Holten's cunney-hole here. Best we make 'em right at home and show them a good time, hey?"

Before they could make the least physical protest, the Thorne sisters found themselves lying on the pounded dirt floor, flat on their backs, heels in the air and their clothes flying. Grunting like hogs in rut, the big, dirty, hairy men took turns defiling them with hard, knobby organs of lust. Outside, the storm became a deluge, a tempest, a maelstrom of incredible violence.

Nature alone saved the girls from the worst. Few of the eighteen outlaws had the stamina to complete the act with all five Thornes. When the last one, a randy kid of sixteen, finished with Helen Thorne, Al Handy rubbed his hands together in appreciation of their pleasant orgy.

181

"Okay, boys. Now I want you five to take these li'l gals to Mr. Wade in Pierre. Might be he'll find a use for them."

Smirking at the shattered, degraded girls, and buoyed by their good fortune, the five indicated hardcases, including the youth with the most stamina, started to prepare for their happy task.

They had been riding day and night for three days now. To Eli Holten it began to feel like he had always been slamming endlessly about Dakota Territory in the saddle. Word had come, during the big council that had insured peace with the Sioux, that another village, this time one of mixed Sioux and Cheyenne who could not live the reservation life, had been attacked near the fork of the Cheyenne and Belle Fourche rivers. Smoke still rose from a burning lodge when Holten and the cavalry arrived there.

A tall, lean, darkly bronzed Cheyenne greeted them, his face a mass of deep parentheses from the smile he wore. "I knew I would be seeing you soon when I talked to the girls who had your necklace, Tall Bear," he spoke to Holten in the Lakota tongue.

"Spotted Hawk, you have me at a disadvantage. The, ah, Thorne girls are not with me. We have been fighting the white pillagers on the Rosebud."

Spotted Hawk's face changed, his eyebrows rising. "They attack on the reservation now? You see, friend. There is no safety in being penned up like the white man's cattle."

Holten refrained from an involved explanation of the distinction between ordinary times and the unusual circumstances of the present. Besides, the Lakota tongue lacked words for some of the more sublime and esoteric aspects of BIA policy. Perhaps, he considered, it was why most Indians didn't trust the bureau responsible for their lives. He settled for some insight into what had happened in the smoking village.

"What brings you here and what happened?"

Spotted Hawk shrugged, a very white man gesture. "What would you expect? The white-eye interlopers who have profaned our sacred Black Hills now openly attack the People anywhere. I came, looking for men to join me. I will not lay aside my weapons until this is ended."

Holten sighed. Quickly he described the events on the Rosebud and at Pine Ridge, then offered a suggestion. "Why don't you join us, then? We're charged by General Corrington to remove the whites from treaty land."

"We might as well. I have five hands of men. We had camped close by and hoped to increase our strength. Then the whites came, burning and killing. We drove them off, killed one hand and three. There are men of my Dog Soldier society in this camp. They will join you, too."

"Good. Then that's settled. We'll start out in the morning."

Twinkling brightly, so far, far away, the multitude of pinpricks in the ebon dome of sky offered faint illumination on the small camp along the infrequently traveled secondary road to Pierre, Dakota Territory from the west. A rock ring and lean-tos made of blankets and India rubber ground clothes blocked any significant light from where the wretched girls lay huddled on a single sheet of rubberized canvas, a thin blanket spread over them.

"We've got to do something about escaping," Doreen whispered to her sisters.

"Sure, but what?" Samantha asked.

"Think, Sam. We can't make a break in daytime;

183

they'd just ride us down. So it has to be at night, and we have to be sure they won't be able to come after us."

"So what?" Helen asked with short temper. "You've always got the big ideas. What about now?"

"Easy," Doreen breathed out quietly. "I do happen to have a plan."

"I knew it," Helen groaned. "I can hardly wait. Oh, tell us, sister with the big mouth. If you'd kept Eli's name out of it, maybe I wouldn't have the sorest muffin in the country."

"Don't be snotty, Helen. It wasn't one of them outlaws who was yellin', 'Oh, deeper, harder,' my dear," Doreen reminded her cattily.

"Shut your face and tell us," Helen snipped.

"If I shut up . . . ooh, hell, listen close."

Their whispers grew more intense, with each adding embellishment to Doreen's idea. At last they could contain their enthusiasm no longer. Giggles broke out, attracting the attention of their captors. Two of the hard, violent young men started their way. In spite of it all, Helen still complained.

"But, dang it, my muffin still feels like fire inside."

Giggling all the more, her sisters began to put on the charm for the gape-mouthed outlaws. "Come on here with us, Sugar," Doreen cooed to the spike-haired towhead with the vacuous grin of a dolt. "I didn't get to tell you before, but I sure loved the way you made use of me the other night. I was thrilled, downright thrilled."

"Oooh, Ben," Samantha warbled to the other hardcase. "You got me all wet and burnin', thinkin' of what you got behind those jeans. Why don't you drop 'em and let's have us some real fun?"

"Aaaah, me—me, too, someone? Won't you come and love me?" Melissa twittered.

Before long each had a randy outlaw between her legs. Each knew it wouldn't take too long. They had arranged to have on hand something hard enough to

184

do a fair job of hitting.

Deservedly pleased with their accomplishments, the detachment that had ridden out with Eli Holten rejoined the main column. When Eli and Lieutenant Fuller reported to Lieutenant Colonel Mayberry, the commander of the 12th delivered the bad news.

"They just . . . slipped out of camp, Eli. I'm sorry. I sent out a detail, but they lost the track. They forded a river in flood from the spring rains and it"—Mayberry paused, then shrugged—"carried them somewhere."

Unprepared for the stunning effect the news had on him, Eli could not frame the questions he wanted to ask. "Are they . . . dead then?"

Mayberry frowned. "That's what aggravates the most. We don't know."

"There's one thing we do know," Major Gratton, the regimental executive officer injected. "This rabble we've been stirring up and ordering out of the Black Hills is getting organized. They've joined this 'militia' the governor has called for. Their stated goal is to drive all the Indians out of the territory. Here, look at these." He handed Holten recent copies of the three major territorial newspapers.

GOVERNOR TO ACTIVATE TERRITORIAL MILITIA
HOSTILES TO BE DRIVEN OUT
ANOTHER BLACK HILLS MASSACRE

Eli Holten read the grim, black headlines while deep furrows formed on his forehead. An angry shake of his head caused his collar-length yellow curls to ripple when he scanned the details under the bold-face banners.

"Governor Delevan Stratton today signed a proclamation establishing a Territorial Militia with a strength of twelve hundred men. Names as Comman-

185

dant of the Militia, with the rank of brigadier general, is prominent territorial businessman, Amos Wade. The governor assures all territory citizens that the savage depredations of hostile Indians will soon be ended. Asked why he has taken such an unprecedented step, the governor replied, "With the army unable or unwilling to perform its duties to protect the citizens of this fair territory, it has become obvious that we must act to protect ourselves. It has come to my attention that the army is in fact protecting the perpetrators of these atrocities, and that soldiers have actually fired on white men, in defense of the hostiles. You can be assured that I have sent strongly worded protests to the general commanding the Military Division of the Missouri. Until those responsible for these heinous crimes are brought to account by their military superiors, our brave militia will stand between the white population and the red menace."

Holten shuddered. For all the rising anger, he could not avoid a thin, cold chill that coursed his spine. He moistened his lips and nodded to the purple prose. "Amos Wade? If it hadn't been for appointing Wade to command the militia, I'd think the governor had lost his mind. Instead, it's only the last vermin crawling out from under the rock."

"We also know where they're forming this militia," Lieutenant Colonel Mayberry informed Eli. "In the Black Hills, naturally. One of the articles you didn't read talks about forcing the 'hostile forces on the reservations' to move westward, presumably far enough not to pose a threat. I don't know what they expect our troops on the agencies to do. Their officers have their orders, and even rookies know how to shoot."

Fleetingly a smile flickered on Eli's lips. "It could prove interesting if we just stood back and let it happen. How long can this collection of untrained, undisciplined drunks, rowdies and saddle tramps stand against a military force *and* the Sioux?"

Mayberry grunted. "Too many people would die. And what might happen if the Sioux got too big a taste for blood again?"

"You've got a point. So, what do we do?" Eli asked.

"We march on them at once. Your Cheyenne, ah-er, auxiliaries will be allowed to accompany us and serve as scouts and, ummm-ah, irregulars."

"Why, thank you, Colonel. Spotted Hawk will be pleased," Holten responded with a light touch of sarcasm.

Holten's levity deserted him late in the afternoon of the next day, fading away with Spotted Hawk and his Cheyenne warriors. Disappointed, Holten grudgingly dismissed them for his considerations as he joined the other officers for a final briefing.

"We'll circle wide of the encampment," Lt. Colonel Howard Mayberry directed. "The camp has been poorly chosen. There's a steep escarpment to the north, a flood-crested river to the east and we'll be to their south and west. Remember, try not to kill any of them. Shoot to frighten them into surrender or to wound. Once the regiment is deployed, we'll attack an hour before sundown."

"What if they take their shootin' seriously?" Lieutenant Fuller asked.

Slowly a smile bloomed on Mayberry's thin lips. "Why, that's what that battery of two six-inch mortars and the Gatling gun in the wagon are for."

CHAPTER 18

Woodpeckers rattled the trees around the militia encampment. Shortly after Lieutenant Colonel Howard Mayberry and his escort rode down into the clearing, and he began to read the formal, army order from General Corrington, commanding their immediate disbanding, bullets began to rattle the trees. Snipers opened up from well-chosen locations. Although wounded, Lieutenant Colonel Mayberry managed to ride back to his lines and order an immediate attack.

On foot, due to the thick growth of fir and lodgepole pine in this portion of the Black Hills, the cavalry steadily advanced. They fired their Springfield carbines in tempo with their march, every time their left feet touched the ground. From the militia encampment came an irregular crackle of gunfire.

"Steady now, shoot high. Shoot high," the sergeants reminded their troops.

When they reached the edge of the clearing, the order came to halt. Horse holders came forward, and the troops began to remount. Right then a mounted force from the militia raced toward them, taking deadly aim. Two soldiers fell wounded, another joined them. One trooper uttered a short, high wail and fell dead. A private designated as company messenger rushed back to Lieutenant Colonel Mayberry.

Expression dark and thunderous, Mayberry heard him out, then issued a quick command. "Go back and tell Captain Melvern to hold fast at the edge of the woods." He returned the messenger's salute and watched the man hurry away. Then, "Mortars, you have four rounds to lay your pieces. Commence firing."

A loud whoosh, like the rush of a dozen freight trains, arced across the sky. "What the fuck was that?" one miner volunteer asked a moment before a huge gout of earth rose skyward and the loud blast assaulted his ears.

"Jee-eesus, I don't know," his companion answered in awe. "Only I hope it don't get any closer."

The next mortar bomb did, bursting some fifty yards to their front. The two miners felt their bowels turn to jelly. "Oh, Christ, what is it?" one wailed.

Moments later the third round landed thirty feet behind, in a line of wagons drawn up side to side, with cataclysmic results. A thousand rounds of ammunition and five hundred pounds of dynamite went off by sympathetic detonation. Men howled and screamed and clutched at aching ears. The ground grumbled and undulated like an earthquake. Horses galloped around wildly, shrieking in mindless terror. A thick pall of dust rose everywhere. Thirty seconds later, two more bombs came crashing in.

In a minute, two more dropped, then another pair. The not-too-orderly camp of the ragtag Territorial Militia became a bedlam of fire, smoke and terror. Men and animals erupted, shattered by blasts and shredded by shrapnel. Only those already in the saddle and engaging the stubborn line at the edge of the trees escaped the carnal madhouse.

"Spread out, spread out!" a junior officer of the militia, with past experience in combat, bellowed. "We're in a mortar attack. Get your horses and ride

189

toward the enemy's main line of resistance."

"Now, would the loo-tenant be so kind as to point out to us where the fuck that might be?" one laconic prospector drawled.

"Out there," he yelled, pointing to the dazzle of muzzle flashes along the L-shaped line of the attackers.

"Now, me," one of the prospectors said, shaking his head, "I was thinkin' of takin' a little swim. What about you, Pard?"

"Sounds like a fine idea to me. Better'n gettin' shot at."

Livid with anger at their talk of deserting, the young officer smashed one in the face with a fist. "I'll shoot you both if you don't get off your asses and charge the enemy."

For his efforts, both of them shot him. While the lieutenant died, troops of the 12th completed the task of dragging forward a wheeled caisson with a long, horizontal object mounted on top, covered by canvas. They set the trails and unveiled their prize with an efficiency of movement that spoke of long practice. Despite the terror and confusion of the mortar attack, Al Handy and several others managed to regain control of the mounted militia and organized a charge on the short arm of the "L."

One of the crew affixed a long, heavy box magazine to the top of the multi-barreled weapon in time to greet the attacking horsemen. The gunner rocked the crank handle backward to prime the Gatling and then began to turn it in a clockwise motion. The device rattled and clanked for a moment, then bellowed loudly in a continuous stream of .45-70 rounds.

Empty casings rang musically as they bounced off the caisson, the sound lost in the stuttering roar of the rapid-firing gun. Men and horses screamed and crashed to the ground. Swiftly the survivors withdrew. From the long flank, the crew of the Gatling gun heard a mighty roar as the opposing forces met head on.

Still under the admonition to try to spare lives, the soldiers used clubbed carbines instead of side arms and cold steel. The heated contest continued for twenty minutes before the militia began to give ground. Cursing the abandonment of the Cheyenne under his breath, Eli Holten went hurriedly from place to place along the battle line. He had nothing to do, other than fight when necessary, and bleakly considered himself useless. Bullets snapped through the trees, releasing a shower of leaves and twigs. If only he had a mobile force, like Spotted Hawk's Cheyenne, to sweep around the far end of the short flank and strike the enemy's command post, he muttered to himself. Cheering rose again when the main forces disengaged.

"We could go on fighting over the same ground for days," Lieutenant Colonel Mayberry complained at the staff meeting. "One concerted push ought to do it. With covering fire from the mortars and Gatling gun we should carry their best resistance in no time. After all, they're rabble, unused to fighting together."

"You couldn't tell it from the way they fought so far," one of the company commanders jibed.

"Never mind that. We'll attack in force in fifteen minutes. There's only half an hour before dark."

Whistles blew and bugles sounded. The 12th Cavalry advanced under the swish and roar of mortar bombs and the stuttering crack of the Gatling gun. They hit the enemy situated among a jumble of rocks halfway across the glade. Men on both sides fought desperately until sundown found them still engaged in hand-to-hand struggles. Nightfall found the battle unresolved.

Burt Sands slapped dust from the front of his coat, then stomped across the narrow wooden porch to the door. He knocked once and was admitted to the tumble-down, waterfront shack in Pierre. Seated at a rickety table, drinking steadily from a bottle of Old Forester, were Zack Walters and two men he had never seen before.

"Where's Amos Wade? I got two more men outside. We gotta talk to him."

Zack blinked and studied Sands closely. Burt showed signs of hard travel, his face gaunt, lined with exhaustion, and he spoke with a thick tongue. He swayed when he tried to stand straight.

"You look awful. What happened to you?" Walters demanded.

"That's what I gotta talk to Mr. Wade about."

"Amos is not here. He's out with his new militia, in the Black Hills."

The news gave Sands a befuddled expression. "We'then, we ain't gonna—gonna make it that far. Best tell you. Al sent sent us. We come across five women, girls really, who said they was friends of Eli Holten. Al sent us an' two others to you with the girls. Only—only we didn't make it."

"Why not?" Walters demanded. "You're here."

"Yeah. Me'n two others. Young Peter Ellis an' Greasy Dick Lane are dead. Them—them little bitty girls screwed our nuts off, then klonked us alongside the head. Only they hit them boys too hard. Then they took all the horses and escaped."

"*Whaaat!*" It was a strangled roar. "Goddammit. Your pricks got in the way of our having valuable hostages. We'd have had Holten in the palm of one hand with them. Jesus, Amos will be furious. All right, all right," Walters began to calm. "Go get cleaned up. Get something to eat and rest up. Then I want you to take a dozen men and go after those girls.

Dawn found the battlefield static. Over night several unsuccessful probes by both sides had been attempted. They left nothing unchanged. Eli Holten stood sipping

192

coffee and gazing toward the enemy lines, now reinforced with piled dirt entrenchments. Beside him, Lieutenant Colonel Howard Mayberry blew on his tin cup and worked his mouth as though trying to dislodge something unpleasant.

"We're cavalry, dammit," the CO of the 12th snapped. "Those breastworks look nasty. The only way to take them is to ride right over the top."

"It can be done," Eli suggested. "Lower the mortars' aim point to drop rounds right on the defenses. Then charge and have the cover fire lifted only seconds before hitting them."

Mayberry pursed his lips. "Mighty risky. A short round could play hell with my men."

"Any other way would lose you a lot more," Holten maintained.

Sighing, Lieutenant Colonel Mayberry clapped Eli Holten on the back. "You always did have a sound tactical mind. Agreed. We'll do it that way. What sort of diversion do you have in mind to take attention off a frontal attack?"

"In this sort of terrain, there's damned little we can do to make it a surprise. Unless . . ." Holten paused, sniffed, then wet a finger. He raised it above his head. "Ummm. That'll be up in an hour or two. Right brisk, I'd say. And it's blowing in the right direction. Before the troops ride out of the woods, we'll fire the grass and let it burn about three-quarters of the way toward them."

Mayberry looked doubtful. "It's mighty green."

"There's enough tall, dead stuff from last year above the spring growth to carry it. At least it will serve to provide a lot of smoke. Behind that we can maneuver anywhere you want."

"We'll do it, by God," Lieutenant Colonel Mayberry enthused.

"Jesus, Al, the whole valley is afire," Lane Parker

told Handy in a rush.

"Does Wade, uh, General Wade know?"

"If he's got eyes, he does. What do we do?" Parker appealed.

"How did it start?"

"I don't know."

"Find out if someone does. I'll go tell General Wade."

Five minutes later, Amos Wade had assembled his officers. At his side stood a thoroughly frightened Mason Ashford. "Gentlemen, this is the beginning of the end. I want enough men left on the line to hold the army while the rest of us swim the river and get the hell out of here. Pick the poorest men, Al, not any of yours. They'll, ah, need some assurance of our continued support. So, someone will have to remain with them." He paused and looked around the gathered leaders. "You, Mason. You'll be ideal for that requirement."

"No! It's unthinkable. It's—it's suicide. You can't make me do that."

Wade produced a sardonic smile that added menace to his cold, implacable features. "You'll stay and do as I tell you, or I'll break your leg and leave you behind."

Shells rained down at the rate of three a minute from each of the mortar guns. Swallowed by the din of constant explosions, the cavalry formed double files abreast and started forward at a trot from their previous lines. Lumbering along behind them, pulled by hand, the Gatling gun caisson came on, to be repositioned at the spine of jumbled boulders. It opened fire immediately, spraying death through the obscuring smoke that masked all sight of the enemy.

Gray-white billows also prevented the enemy from seeing the advancing troops. At a distance of a hundred yards, Lieutenant Colonel Mayberry gave a silent arm signal changing the gait to a gallop. The last two mortar bombs whooshed overhead.

"Trumpeter, sound the Charge!" Mayberry bellowed.

For all their preparations, the outlaw militia broke at once. The bugle notes cut at them, sharp, crystal and appallingly close. How had the army gotten there? Abandoning the breastworks, they fled. Here and there men fought as individuals, or in desperate clots of three to eight. The cavalry swept in among them howling, .45 Smith & Wesson Scoffields blazing. Reverted to a mob, the terrified riffraff began to back up an incline, perforce being pushed closer together.

Nearness brought a false sense of security, and their firing became less erratic. They began to inflict serious losses on the troops. Rallied by their success, many uttered a brief cheer and doubled their efforts at resistance. The attack had not been nearly so terrible, they told themselves and each other. Nor had the sheer escarpment been that difficult to scale. At the top, even Mason Ashford had taken heart. They would go over the crest and take cover. From there they could pot-shot the soldiers, who had been forced to dismount to follow.

Only a handful of hastily appointed officers took note of a sudden clatter and rattle of stones behind them. Their jubilation fled when the sound became louder and they turned to see what made it.

Long lines of Sioux and Cheyenne warriors, three files deep, armed and spoiling for revenge, covered the backslope. Yelling in terror, Mason Ashford started the mass rush to surrender to the cavalry. Smiling in satisfied amusement, Spotted Hawk rode forward and waved to Eli Holten.

"I am a thpethial réprethentative of the governor. I demand to be releathed at onthe." Mason Ashford's lisp irritated Eli Holten long before he came into sight.

"Everything's secured, Colonel," Eli informed Mayberry. "The Cheyenne Dog Soldiers will scout for anyone who escaped, while the Sioux serve as pickets. Who's this bird of bright plumage?"

"Mason Ashford," Mayberry informed him before walking away.

Ashford stood in leg irons and manacles, dirty and powder begrimed, his hair and gaudy clothing awry. He had a sullen, defeated expression, and his oddly colored eyes had gone flat with despair. Then a faint flicker of recognition glowed, grew, and flamed as he concocted a scheme for self-preservation.

"You're Eli Holten, aren't you?" he chirped.

"I am. What difference does that make?"

"I have it on good authority that you are intimately acquainted with five young women, girls actually, named Thorne. Melissa, Doreen, Samantha, Susanna and Helen?"

Holten scowled. "What if I am?"

"I also know that underlings of Al Handy captured them some short while ago and amused themselves with the tender young things' bodies. After which, Al sent them off to his masters in Pierre. Al Handy escaped your nasty little trick with the Indians, you know. He and Amos Wade got off entirely unharmed, along with about fifteen others. I'm sure you can visualize what is going to happen to those sweet little girls when Handy and Wade get back to Pierre," he concluded in as much of a sneer as a frightened captive could muster.

With balled fists, Holten snapped a hard, straight right that knocked the unarmed Mason Ashford to the ground. Following through, Holten leaped on Ashford, fists punishing the frail young man's ribs.

"Corporal of the Guard, Post Number Six, a fight is in progress," the startled sentry standing watch on Ashford shouted.

It took the entire off-duty guard mount to wrest Eli Holten's death grip from Mason Ashford's scrawny,

196

scratched and reddened throat. Shivering and snorting with anger, Holten growled at the men who restrained him.

"Let me at him. I want to finish it. I'll beat the truth out of that sissy rag mop."

Gradually the first explosion of rage subsided. Holten went to Lieutenant Colonel Mayberry. He wanted to take off at once and go look for the missing girls.

"I'm sorry, Eli. That won't be possible. Orders from Frank, if I have to pull that into it. You are to stay with the column until we return to Fort Rawlins."

Conscience-searing worry delivered the words, not the deep affection for his old friend. "And I came all the way from Arizona for this." He sighed heavily and went to find Sonny. They had a lot of miles to cover.

CHAPTER 19

Tears wetted the thick, auburn lashes of Melissa Thorne's eyes. There before them, shining in the sunlight of a new spring day, stood the palisades of Fort Rawlins. They had made it. At last they had reached the goal set so long ago. No. It had only been a matter of two weeks. So little time?

"Eli will be there," she broke the silence to assure her sisters. "By now they have to be back. If we could trick those dumb ol' outlaws, they couldn't stand long against the army."

"Much as I want to believe that, sister dear," Doreen, ever practical, delivered gloom. "But, if you give it some thought, I'm sure you'll agree; those soldiers don't have exactly the same weapon to use as we have."

Giggles banished Melissa's tears. She prodded her horse in the ribs and took the lead toward the tall, main gate. Behind her, Helen groaned.

"I don't think I'll ever be able to close my legs again."

Samantha looked at her youngest sister with the tip of one index finger supporting her chin. "Why ever would you want to?"

More titters of mirth buoyed them along the last precious mile. Disappointment waited when they arrived. First off they were told they would have to make camp outside the walls of the fort. They protested, using Eli Holten's name. When that only brought further challenge, Doreen claimed that they were relatives of the scout. That got them an interview with Colonel Britton.

"You are nieces of Eli Holten?" the portly, impressive officer challenged when Doreen finished her fanciful tale.

"Oh, yes, sir, yes indeed. Surely he's told you about his dear sister Ruth?"

Britton scratched at the lobe of one ear. "I don't believe he has."

"Why, I never. Though I suppose in his profession Uncle Eli is a close-mouthed sort, isn't he?"

"Ummmm," Britton allowed noncommitally. "Well, at least we can let you stay in his cabin. It's located on Officers' Row. Number Twenty-eight. You can find it easily enough. The officers' wives will show you where to draw water and get firewood. You can draw rations on a chit until Eli returns."

"Oh, bless you, Colonel, sir," Doreen cooed, rising on tiptoe to give his cheek a chaste peck.

"Uh-hummm—er-ummm, yes, yes, go along now girls."

Moments later, Melissa exploded in feminine disgust. "You mean he *lives* in *this?* Ugh, it's awful."

"Smells musty," Doreen contributed.

"It's a mess," Helen summed up.

Typical of most confirmed bachelors, Eli Holten gave less than passing attention to the appearance of his quarters. He had only occupied this square, two-room cabin on Officers' Row for three nights before the 12th deployed into the field. It had been enough to put the single male stamp on it. Soiled clothing lay in heaps or dangled from chair backs. Dirty dishes, some with dried crusts of their former contents, spilled into the sink. Coffee, in a granite pot on the combination cooking-heater wood stove, grew a beard of black and green on its scummy surface. Melissa and her sisters sighed in resignation and stumbled into the modest dwelling.

Dust fogged the windows; industrious spiders had created festoons of gossamer bunting along where the ceiling joined with the walls, with more spreading fanlike in the corners of the doorcasing between the main room and bedroom. A gray-brown haze, of neglect covered everything. Bemoaning the peculiarities of the male animal, all males, the Thorne sisters improvised aprons and set to work righting the masculine wrongs. Their manic energy and single-minded determination to "pretty things up" would have made Eli Holten want to puke.

"We'll have it so nice when he gets back," Melissa burbled.

"I can sew curtains, nice ones of chintz. And a slipcover for that broken-down ol' stuffed leather chair," Doreen offered.

"They'll make us leave here," Samantha stated gloomily as she gathered bedding and clothes for the laundry.

"Why, Sam? Eli'll want us to stay; I just know he will," Melissa burbled.

"There's five of us and only one of him. A man can't have five wives. We'll have to go out Utah or Idaho way; the Mormons understand that sort of thing," Samantha displayed her worldly knowledge, gleaned from her father's books.

"So what if we do?" Helen asked, undisturbed. "At least we'll be together."

A knock at the outside door interrupted their enthusiastic gabble. "Hello, I'm Martha Gower. Captain Gower is my husband. Eleventh infantry? Has your father been stationed here?"

"Uh—no, ma'am. We—we-re Eli Holten's nieces," Doreen informed her.

A single frown line creased Martha Gower's high, smooth brow. "Oh, I see."

"Yes, ma'am. We'll be here awhile, and we thought the first thing would have to be to clean up this terrible mess. Phew! Men just can't keep house."

Apprehensions melted away, and Martha beamed at the five lovely young women. "How true that is. Eli Holten had these quarters when he was assigned here and—well, him being your uncle and all, I hesitate to—"

"It's always been a rat's nest." Melissa made it easy for her.

Martha gave off a trill of laughter. "That's it, exactly. A disgrace, if you know what I mean. I'm so happy to see someone undertake to rectify it."

"We'll sure try, ma'am," Samantha piped up.

"Please, call me Martha. Is there anything you need?"

"We could use some lye soap," Melissa began listing, "and water, lots of water, and we need to know how to fill out the form for Quarters Allowance."

"I think I can help you with all of that." Martha turned away to call outside the cabin. "Oh, Jimmy, Jimmy, come here, son."

A clatter of shoe leather on hard-packed earth announced the approach of Jimmy Gower. He hit the open doorway with arms and legs akimbo and stopped his headlong motion by grasping the jamb. "Yes, Momma?"

Big, melting blue eyes looked up from under a fringe of soft, light brown hair, cut in bangs that covered a high, smooth forehead. The slender, small-statured, fresh-faced thirteen-year-old shifted his gaze to the auburn-haired splendor of the five lovely Thorne sisters, and his features formed a sappy, bemused expression.

"Jimmy, I want you to run next door and fetch a big hunk of my lye soap. Bring it here so that these dear girls can start cleaning out this midden heap."

Jimmy Gower wrinkled his button nose. "Eli won't

201

like that," he observed.

"Now, Jimmy," Martha admonished. "It's long overdue and you know it. You hurry along now. Then you can take one of them to the well and show her where to draw water."

"Awh, Momma, Corey an' Eddie Sparks an' I were shootin' marbles," Jimmy started to protest. Then his sweet nature shined through, and he produced a beaming flash of white. It quickly faded behind lips that were sensuously full at the mid-line, forming an enthralling bow, before they thinned to mere dark lines at the edges of his mouth which turned up in a perpetual smile.

"Okay, Momma," Jimmy chirped, using the latest slang.

He came back in no time, a huge chunk of creamy yellow lye soap clutched in one hand. Shyly he held it out to Helen and lowered long, nearly blond lashes over his startling azure eyes when their fingers managed to touch. Still in charge, his mother spoke crisply.

"Now grab up those buckets and help with the water, son."

"Yes, ma'am."

"I'll go," Helen volunteered hastily.

Samantha and Susanna tittered behind hastily positioned hands. Mrs. Gower appeared not to notice. Helen and Jimmy started off for the well.

"If you'll come with me, we'll go to the commissary sergeant and draw your Quarters Allowance," Martha said to Melissa.

"Fine, we'll both go," Melissa accepted, with a glance to Doreen.

With their sisters gone, Sam and Susie set off to explore Officers' Row and get their bearings. So, when Helen returned with Jimmy, two brimming wooden buckets slopping water over their rims, they found the house empty. A warm glow came alive in Helen's eyes, and she sat on a dusty sofa—the gift of a long-ago departing lieutenant's wife—and patted the space beside her.

"Jimmy, put down those buckets and come sit with me. Tell me about the fort."

Jimmy Gower squirmed in confusion born of painful innocence. He wore clothes of a style unlike any the Thorne sisters had ever seen before. A pair of knickers had been salvaged from their raggedy state by his mother, cut off and hemmed so that they ended a bit above mid-thigh. Although thin, his well-browned bare legs rippled with muscle and only fueled the low flame that warmed Helen's loins. The sleeves had been removed from his collarless shirt, baring his arms, which added yet another titillation to the precocious girl. Insistently, eager now, she rapped the cushion again, producing a large poof of dust. They both giggled, and Jimmy sat beside her.

The youngsters talked for the better part of half an hour, then Helen could stand it no longer. "Oh, Jimmy, you're so *cute*," she simpered as she placed a warm, soft hand on one bare thigh and began to slide it up toward his crotch.

Jimmy shied at the touch, flushed pinkly, and produced a puzzled grin. Helen asked another question and advanced farther toward her goal. Jimmy squirmed and swung the affected leg from side to side. Undeterred, Helen took the final, irreversible leap. Jimmy let out a little squeak when she reached her objective and gave him a little squeeze.

"Wh-why did you want to do that?" he gulped. Then he discovered that what he had long believed to be a dormant object, suitable only for bodily elimination, had a life of its own. It caused him to writhe in discomfort and embarrassment. Yet, it tingled and felt rather nice.

"Helen!" Doreen squawked from the doorway.

Springing apart in confusion, the two youngsters looked up in contrasting expression; Jimmy startled,

203

Helen trying to mask her arousal.

"Oh, my, how time flies," Helen bolted out. "My, my."

"We, ah, have some, ah, family matters to discuss. Can you come back later, Jimmy?" Doreen suggested.

"Oh, ah, sure—sure. I—I'd like that." He shot a shy glance at Helen.

Helen stared dewy-eyed after him as he departed. "I'm in love," she crooned.

"You're in *lust* is more like it," Doreen grumped. "That poor boy is so innocent you're liable to give him a heart seizure."

"But, oh, Reenie, he's soooo sweeet," Helen rhapsodized. "Why, he doesn't even know what his little dingus is for."

"And you're only too eager to teach him, eh?" Doreen added cattily. "Well, little Miss Muffin, you had better mind your manners, or someone is likely to take you over his knee and spank your butt."

"He-he's sooo cuuuute," Helen wailed. "I can make him sooo happy."

"Remember who we came here to see," Doreen warned.

"Oh . . . yes . . . Eli," Helen choked out.

DISASTER IN THE BLACK HILLS!

Governor Delevan Stratton slammed the newspaper down on the table in a private suite of the ornate, perfume-scented bordello in Pierre so that Amos Wade could read the headlines. The army's intervention and the humiliation of the militia had drawn the corrupt politician out of his lair in a fury. He shook a fist in momentary frustration and glowered at Wade.

"You might as well died there with the rest," the governor snarled.

"I fail to see the advantage in that," Amos Wade said

204

coolly, his inner self boiling with trepidation. He and Al Handy had escaped by only the narrowest of margins.

"The advantage is that our little secret would have died with you. Now, if the army mixes further into this, I'll find myself rotting in Leavenworth."

"Which condition is considerably preferable to swinging on a gallows. That would be the ultimate fate for me, Al and Zack here if the army does push it. I would be less concerned about my precious little hide, and more about protecting your fellow conspirators, were I you."

"You can't gain anything by threatening me," Governor Stratton blustered.

Wade's flat, frigid stare propelled severe chills along Stratton's spine. "No. That's not a threat. If it meant escaping the rope, I'd turn you in to them in an instant."

"My God, man, you can't mean that. What do we— what can we do about it?"

Wade smiled bleakly. "That's better, your Excellency. We have to close off all channels that might lead to us. Eliminate everyone who can put this together. Too bad about your loyal assistant, but Ashford's one less mouth we have to stopper. Only two people can put together enough to endanger us. Eli Holten is one, Frank Corrington the other. Al is going to see that this time they are disposed of before any harm can be done."

After days of riding, Eli Holten and the troops returned to Fort Rawlins in a mildly triumphant state. They brought along some thirty prisoners, among them Mason Ashford. The governor's private secretary had been babbling about the conspiracy since recovering from Eli's powerful fists. All of it had been dutifully noted by a patient clerk from the regimental headquarters company. While the officers went through the standard routine of dictating or writing their reports of the action, Eli headed for Frank Corrington's hospital room.

He found the general sitting up in bed, his back propped by three huge, fat, goose-feather pillows. Corrington's face brightened like a gaslight globe when Holten entered the room.

"Word of your success preceded you, Eli. Congratulations."

"Thanks, Frank. But . . . I'm afraid it isn't over as yet. The big boys slipped out of the net. We had them. But they took advantage of our last attack to sneak away across the river."

"Headed where?" the general queried.

"Where else? They no doubt feel quite safe going about business as usual in Pierre after the slaughter in the Black Hills. They represented the only persons, close to being captured, who could put the whole thing together. Naturally, they had to assume Mason Ashford would be killed in the final assault. In fact, there's strong evidence that they had arranged for exactly that with one of Al Handy's gunhawks. His point of aim appeared to be the side of Ashford's head when I knocked him off his feet."

"If your horse ran him down, he can be questioned," Corrington suggested.

Holten shook his head. "I knocked him off his feet with a blow from my tomahawk, which split his skull from crown to chin."

"Damn. We're tending to lose too many sources of information on this one, Eli."

The scout shrugged. "Fortunes of combat, Frank. Anyway, all that remains to be done is clean up this nest of snakes."

"Ashford's been quite helpful?"

"He's said enough to get a dozen men hanged. I propose to rest up over night, then get a start for Pierre

206

in the morning. I want to take along Corporal Newcomb and a couple of his Crow scouts."

"How about a platoon? Odds are some of the militia will be on hand to protect the bosses."

"We might as well go in with the brigade band blaring," Holten protested. Before he could add more, an orderly entered with a cloth-draped tray.

"Compliments of Mr. Holten," he announced, whisking away the covering.

He revealed a bottle of General Corrington's favorite brandy and a cedar box of fine, hand-rolled cigars. He poured neatly and handed each man a glass, then offered the tobacco. Holten looked closely at the man. It wasn't the orderly to whom he had given the instructions. Yet, he'd been away a long while and spent little time in the garrison since returning. Replacements came and went. Eli relaxed and lifted his glass to the general.

"To an end of this, Frank."

"Amen to that."

Quietly the orderly let himself out of the room. Holten brought up a new subject. "We have to catch them in such a manner there can be no doubt."

"I see that, of course. To simply tell it the way we see it," Corrington elaborated, "would give some people the idea we'd been smoking loco weed."

"That's the gist of it, Frank. Ashford couldn't help us as to motive. There's simply no reason behind the open provocation of the Indians. At least none that would hold water. Too many chances the government would step in and say the land belonged to the Department of the Interior. No gain, no motive."

"It couldn't be . . . simply revenge on you and me?" Corrington posed.

"I . . . don't think so." He dropped the conversation when the orderly returned with another tray.

Instantaneously Holten's sixth sense detected a certain jerkiness in the hospitalman's movements, a

207

furtive darting of his eyes and a tenseness the scout usually associated with a person caught in a lie, or one compelled to over-control in order not to give away his true purpose. Ei started to speak to him, when the man reached under the towel on his tray.

He came out with a .45 Colt revolver. "Frank!" Holten shouted as he dived out of his chair, hand snake-fast to the butt of his Remington.

Released, the tray made a noisy clatter on the floor a moment before Ei Holten triggered a round that blasted a hole through the assassin's chest. His Colt went flying as Eli cocked his Remington for a safety shot if necessary. The would-be killer uttered a liquid groan and slumped across the end of Corrington's bed. Eli got to him in a second.

"You're dying, you know that," Holten snapped. "Make it easy for yourself on the other side. Tell me who sent you? Why did you try to kill us?"

"Paid—big money. Oh—oh, God it hurts. T-to kill gen'ral an' y-you."

"Who?" Holten all but shouted.

"A-A-Amos. Amos Wade. He an' . . . Gov-Governor Stratton."

"Where are they?"

"Pierre."

"Where in Pierre?"

"D-don't know. Wh-whorehouse, maybe. Fancy place. They sent for me. I—oh! Oooh—no—no—I . . . I . . ."

"He's dead, Eli," Frank Corrington said gently. Holten was shaking the corpse, hoping for something more.

"Now we know for sure. And we have his dying confession. I'll compromise with you, Frank. I'll take two squads. An hour before daylight."

"Fine. And what about your family?"

"Fam—family? I don't have any family, Frank. You know that."

"You do now," Corrington said with a chuckle. "At least that's what the brigade sergeant major tells me. Five lovely young ladies with coppery hair."

Holten groaned and smacked a palm against his forehead. "The . . . Thornes. What the hell are *they* doing here?"

CHAPTER 20

Even a casual observer could tell Eli Holten was hot from the way he stomped across the parade ground. It had taken another hour to go over the killing in Frank Corrington's room. That did little to mollify the scout's mood. He headed for Officers' Row with a thunderous expression that would paralyze a mountain lion. When he burst through the door to his lodging, the Thorne sisters released a communal "Oooh" of dread.

" 'Oh,' indeed," Holten growled. "What do you mean telling everyone we are related? More, what put it in your head to leave the column when I told you to stay put? You know, I had you marked for dead. First from raiding Indians, then from Amos Wade."

"We—we didn't know what else to do," Melissa pleaded ignorance.

"The least you could have done was send a message to the expedition that you had reached the fort safe and alive," Eli said.

"Oh! Yes—yes, I suppose we should have," Doreen inserted.

"And, oh, Eli, we've all decided. We're going to marry you—all of us. All at the same time. We've missed you and been so miserable without you to keep us happy. We'll live together somewhere. Maybe here, if we can; if not, somewhere else."

"Y-y-you what?" Holten stammered.

"Marry you. We're so glad to see you, Eli," Helen burbled. "Do you, ah, do you know anything about that divine little boy next door, Jimmy Gower?"

Holten took one short look at Helen, and his anger turned to helpless exasperation. "I suppose you've been trying to get in his pants?"

"I—I did get in his pants . . . for a little while. Last night." Helen stopped to giggle. "Only . . . only nothing happened." She did a long take, then batted silken copper lashes at Eli Holten, in imitation of virginal naivete.

"Oh, you'd have seen to it something happened, Helen," Holten said acidly, his distemper edging into resignation.

Ignoring the import of his words, Helen blundered on. "Anyway, I've gotten *into* them, even if it took four days of trying, but I haven't gotten him *out of* them as yet. And I thought you might . . . help . . . me!" she ended in a squeak as Holten started for her.

Eli took her waist in one big hand and lifted Helen from the floor. He sat on the newly cleaned sofa and bent her across his knees. With one swift yank he pulled up the hem of her dress, exposing her bloomer-clad buttocks. The thin cloth would be no impediment, Holten gauged. Raising his big, ham hand, he proceeded to deliver her half a dozen swift, hard swats.

Helen howled with a woman's indignation and gulped back a little girl's tears while she endured this humiliation. Slowly she realized that Holten's intimate attack on her buns had the effect of wildly exciting her and arousing her. Twisting her head, she gave him a long, provocative look over her shoulder and slowly licked her lips.

Holten let go of her and grabbed up the twins. They all fell in a tumble on the couch, then Eli began to whale away at their bottoms. While he did, he lectured the startled quintet.

211

"Now, I'm going to tell you what is going to happen. You are going to make ready to depart for your home as soon as the roads are dry enough and it's safe enough to travel."

"Oooh nooo, Eli," all five wailed. "We can't live without you. You've got . . . so much . . . we need so badly."

"Please be our man . . . our *only* man. You promise that, Helen. Swear it, you hear?" Melissa moaned in sincerity.

"Oh, I will," Helen sobbed. "I do, I swear it. I won't even look at Jimmy again, now you're here, Eli."

"Enough!" Eli thundered, dumping the twins to the floor. "Do as I say," he warned. "I'll be back in a week, and I want you gone."

"Where are you going?" the female chorus appealed to him.

"Pierre," he snapped at them as he went out the door.

Eli Holten reached Pierre, Dakota Territory with the images of the three men responsible for all the trouble burned in his memory. Although dead and buried, Hezakiah Manning had been replaced by Governor Delevan Stratton. With the troopers of the 12th to watch for militiamen, Holten set out to search for the evil trio.

While Eli determined that the governor was absent from his office and his home, Al Handy leaned against the bar in the Orient Pearl saloon, nursing his mental wounds. Such ignominious defeat and flight rankled. At the outset he had seen the others' blind hatred of General Corrington and Eli Holten as irrational. Now he clearly saw how it might be reasonably placed. He sipped steadily, if not deeply, from a bottle of Old Overholt rye while he worried about the success of the latest attempt on the lives of Holten and the general. Each time someone entered or left the saloon, one of the batwing door hinges squeaked. It worked havoc on

Al's frayed nerves. The rasping noise came again, and Al turned with a look of anger.

Eli Holten stood framed in the doorway. In the first fleeting instant, Handy realized that their man had failed again. He also knew of only one reason Holten would be there. Al's hand dropped to the hard rubber butt-grips of the .45 Colt at his side. The sixgun came free at the same time Eli Holten drew his Remington. Al Handy fired first.

Like the glancing blow of a hammer, Eli Holten felt the slug rip along the right side of his throat. It left a hot, wet trail that dripped onto his shoulder. In reflex his head had jerked and dislodged his hat. It sailed backward into the street. All the while he triggered his Remington.

Holten's bullet shattered the Old Overholt bottle and sent sprays of liquor and glass in a widening sphere. Returning a second round, Eli lunged forward as Al dived for the floor. From there Al threw a careless shot at Holten that lodged in the shoulder of a bystander. Eli's third shot pinwheeled a brass spitoon which sent it ringing bell-like along the bar. That gave motion to Al Handy, who set off running awkwardly for the narrow hallway to the back door. Eli Holten bounded after him.

In the clear, Eli's fourth try hit Al high in his right hip. The outlaw leader stumbled off balance and slammed into the door. Before Eli could follow up with his last round, Handy wrenched the portal open and disappeared out the back. Reloading, Eli started after him.

He had ejected the fourth empty casing and inserted a fresh cartridge by the time he reached the alley. Eli added a sixth cartridge and looked warily around. No sign of Handy. Blood drops, small, dark-red craters of the moon, led toward the mouth of the alley. Cautiously, Holten let them lead him.

*   *   *

"Goddammit, I tell you he's come after all of us," Al Handy shouted at Amos Wade.

"Then get out there and stop him," Wade grunted.

He reclined on a bed in the gaudily decorated room like a Roman emperor at a banquet, his only covering a rich, burgundy velvet robe that had been pulled open at the front. His strained voice came from the intense pleasure he received from the soiled dove who knelt on the floor, between his legs, giving oral stimulation to his short, fat organ.

"How can I? I'm shot, I'm bleeding," Handy protested.

"Aaaah, that's fine, my dear," he crooned, then spoke to Handy. "Get some of the boys and go out and kill Holten. Do I have to do your thinking for you?"

Unmanned by his pain, Handy nearly sobbed. "I don't know where anyone is. I can't hardly stand up. I . . . dammit, Mr. Wade, Holten's gonna kill us all."

"Ummmm—aaaaah—yeaaah, a little more," Wade panted. "Get ahold of yourself, Handy. You were hired to do the gun work. Now get the hell out there and do it."

Al Handy stumbled from the room. Fuzzy blackness waited at the edges of his vision. His hip throbbed and continued to slowly pump droplets of blood from the wound. He found a dark space under the rear stairs in the hallway. He'd wait there for Eli Holten.

Crimson smears led to the rear door of the biggest, fanciest bordello in Pierre. Eli Holten tried the knob and found it free. He turned it and flung the portal inward. Keeping low, he dived through. No weapons barked, and no slugs raced to greet him. Prone on the carpet runner, Holten made a quick visual survey of his surroundings.

A short distance down the hall, a fresh, crimson stream led from behind the staircase. Nothing else appeared out of place. Cautiously Holten raised to hands and knees and made an awkward dash for the steps. He made it halfway when Al Handy sort of toppled out into the hall. The Colt in Handy's right hand discharged. The slug burned air over Eli's back. Holten repaid the offering.

Al Handy sprang upward to his scant five foot five as he sucked in a deep, violent draught of air. Then he looked downward at the black hole in his middle that leaked a thin trickle of blood from his abdomen. The Colt went slack in his hand for a moment and then swung into position on the tide of new frustration and outrage that drove him beyond the spreading numbness in his gut. With infinite effort, he eared back the hammer.

Eli Holten shot him again, in the chest, ruptured Al's heart and stopped his baneful life forever. Quickly Holten started up the stairs. Shattering glass and loud feminine shrieks informed him the troopers had acted on his hasty instructions. At the first shots, they broke down the door and stormed into the bordello to cover all exits. No one would escape from this place. Swiftly Holten negotiated the remaining risers

Now it became hunting time. Every door presented a risk. At any moment Wade or his henchmen could pop from a room and down Eli in a shredding blast from a shotgun. Hugging one wall, he started along toward the first door on his side.

He heard no sounds behind it, yet took no chances. Feeling terribly vulnerable with only two layers of lath and plaster between him and a bullet, if one came, he shot an inch inward from the keyhole and blasted off the lock case. Impact swung the door open. A feminine scream answered the damage, and it came again when Holten dived through the opening, rolled and came to his feet, the Remington searching the room.

"Ain't nobody here but me, mister," the shop-worn drab who cowered behind the bed pleaded.

Eli Holten made a thorough check anyway. Then he stepped out into the hall. Two hardcases faced him, weapons ready in hand. One had a nervous tic at the corner of his mouth which gave him the appearance of chewing a cud. He made his try first.

He might have been good, at least in some circles, but Eli Holten was much better. The Remington bucked and spat a .44 slug that smashed its nose on the top-strap of the Colt Peacemaker in the outlaw's hand, changed direction and howled sepulchrally as it zipped outward and through the underside of the gunhawk's jaw. His eyes bulged, and he rocked backward, his head in a sphere of crimson mist.

"Die, Holten!" the other gunman snarled.

A slow trickle of blood still seeped from the graze along Eli's neck and distracted him somewhat. His aim remained a slight bit off when he answered the reckless shooter's challenge. Instead of hitting dead-center as intended, Holten's bullet drilled a messy hole through the right side of the gunhawk's chest and cracked his shoulder blade. His sixgun discharged a round into the ceiling, and he went down soundlessly, stunned by pain and shock.

Holten plucked the weapon from numbed fingers, picked up the dead man's gun, and stepped over the bodies. At the next room, he encountered a repetition of the first. Apologizing to the frightened soiled dove, he made his way to the next. Before tackling the unknown, Eli reloaded and checked his reserve supply. Good thing he'd taken the guns from the two hardcases, he thought when he finished the count. It gave him a backup he might need. Readying himself, Holten tried the doorknob.

Three bullets punched through the thin wooden panel. Splinters flew like shrapnel. Two larger ones pierced his shirt and drew blood on his hard, flat abdomen. Wincing at the new source of pain, Holten kicked the door and fired blindly into the room.

Glass tinkled, and a thin cry answered him. "Okay, okay, don't shoot. I give up, don't shoot."

A heavy odor of kerosene permeated the room when Eli entered. The outlaw who had fired at him crouched beside a nightstand, blood streaming down his face from a half dozen cuts. The ruins of an oil lamp covered the top of the little table.

"Get down," Holten commanded. "Face first on the floor. Now!"

Meekly, the gunslinger complied. "Y-you ain't gonna kill me?"

"No," Holten said as he walked over to the prone man.

He holstered his Remington and knelt. Using the outlaw's suspenders, he hog-tied him, making sure of the knots at wrists and ankles and that the elastic material lay smoothly across the gunman's throat. He started to rise when a voice came from the hallway.

"Well, Eli Holten. You saved me the trouble of hunting you down."

Eli looked up into brittle, hate-flickering eyes the color of cold ice. Close-set and red-rimmed from lack of sleep, they gave the impression of something salvaged from a graveyard. Holten recognized Zacharia Walters at once, taken back only a bit by the stylish new Colt Lightning in the open pouch holster that dangled from the malign criminal's cartridge belt.

"Give it up, Walters," Holten said evenly as his powerful legs pistoned him upright. "This place is full of soldiers. Your game's over, whatever it was."

"Oh? You don't know?" Walters laughed. "The land stealing and gold strikes were all window dressing. Our plan, our great plan, had to do with getting a railroad through here. There's millions, hundreds of millions to be made that way. That, and about you and Frank Corrington and ten years in prison. Ten years of hell. I've waited for this moment, dreamed of it, practiced for it. Now I have you. Go for your gun, Holten. Draw!"

Doesn't the fool know that a real gunfighter, a live,

217

successful one, shoots with his gun, not his mouth? Eli Holten believed he should laugh. He also knew Zacharia Walters had to be mad as they came.

"You're insane. You and Wade. Manning's dead, so's Handy. Surrender now and it will go easier on you," Holten ventured.

"I'm not mad!" Walters shrieked. "It's the world that's gone insane. That's another issue. Draw you son of a bitch."

Eli Holten's hand dropped to his Remington. Faintly he heard boots pounding on the stairway. There would be soldiers up here in a moment. His fingers wrapped around the smooth walnut grips. In a startling flash he saw that Walters had the cylinder cleared of leather already. Holten shucked the Model '60 Army in a blur.

Blindingly fast, Walters' Colt Lightning cleared the pocket, and flame lanced from the muzzle. In action-slowed motion, Eli saw his hammer fall. Too late! A fraction too late. He heard the roar of Zack Walters' .44 Colt, then felt the buck of the Remington. His mind ran at high speed while everything else seemed to creep. He didn't have a chance at such short range.

He felt the wind of the bullet as it passed through the loose leather of his buckskin shirt. Hot and stinging, the violated flesh of his armpit protested where the lead had gouged out a chunk of muscle. He saw Walters flinch, his face a fleeting mask of agony. The criminal mastermind took an uncertain step backward, his gaze directed to the .44 Lightning in his hand, expression disbelieving. Walters opened his mouth, and a torrent of blood gushed out. His skin turned a sickly gray-green, and he sagged to the floor, a final, ghostly grunt heralding his way into eternity.

"Mr. Holten! Are you all right, sir?" a young soldier's called from the hallway.

"I'm . . . fine. Now we have to go after Amos Wade."

CHAPTER 21

Quiet filled the upper hallway of the elaborate bordello in Pierre. At the far end, toward the street, Eli Holten saw a gilt-edged door made of thick wood, painted white and trimmed in gold leaf, giving it the look of an earlier era. The fat-cheeked, kissing cherubs above the fancy capital clearly came from the rococo period. Recalling Amos Wade's exorbitant taste, Holten knew where he would find the bald man with the cold, hard, flat brown eyes.

"Get some others up here and clean out this rat's nest. I'm going down there," Eli ordered, with a nod to the baroque suite.

Holten tried to kick the door in and damned near broke his ankle. Sharp little pains radiated up to his groin. Using one of the captured .45s, he blasted away the lock mechanism and bashed his way into the suite. Three young women, one of them not as old as Helen Thorne, screamed in terror at his appearance, blood staining his neck, chest and one side. The smoking Colt in his hand did little to reassure them.

"Where is he? Where is Amos Wade?" Holten growled.

"I—I—I . . . we—we—we—" one lovely stammered.

"G-g-g-gone," another blurted.

"Not unless he can fly," Holten grunted. "Come

219

on, tell me."

For a long ten seconds, silence held; one of the girls sobbed. The youngest made a frightened, half-nod toward a large copper bathtub, situated on a marble platform beyond gossamer curtains. Holten gave her a brief, disbelieving stare. Then he walked to the doorway.

Soapy water had splashed onto the marble slab that supported the tub. Someone had gotten out, or in, recently. Eli Holten made a quick check to each side of the opening, then entered. The Colt felt out of balance in his hand. Not the time to change, he reminded himself. The surface of the water, and the piles of suds above it, rippled in a steady rhythm. On tiptoe, Holten approached the steaming container. The water roiled, and a pale, pink whale broached in a shower of droplets.

Holten nearly shot him. Dripping, a patch of bubbles still on the crown of his bald pate, Amos Wade stood before him. He held a thoroughly wet Merwin and Hulbert in his left hand. Mouth working, but unable to produce coherent words, Wade raised the sixgun. Holten triggered the Colt first.

A loud click came from the sixgun when hammer landed on an empty chamber. The Merwin and Hulbert went off with a spectacular effect. Amos Wade howled in pain at the stubs of his severed fingers when the wet cylinder exploded out of the frame. Blood squirted from three stumps.

"Help me," he shrieked. "Oh, God, help me."

Holten had recovered from the nasty surprise the Colt had given him and dropped the gun on the cushion of a loveseat close by. Unwilling to trust Amos Wade, he drew his Remington before he stepped closer to the bath. A tourniquet would staunch the flow of blood, he calculated, and Wade would live to hang. He reached the tub edge, where Wade stood shaken and pallid, his right hand in a towel he held to the mangled left.

Holten reached for it, and pain seared in his fingers as a knife flashed out of the cloth. Reflexively he fired the Remington, angled too high for a solid blow. The bullet ripped off Amos Wade's nose and plowed a deep furrow vertically on his extensive forehead. Impact knocked him unconscious, and Wade fell backward out of the water. His small, pink toes sparkled wetly in a stray beam of sunlight that streamed between closed velvet drapes. From the room behind him, Eli heard choked sobs.

Turning, Eli Holten saw the huddled form of Governor Delevan Stratton kneeling on the living room floor of the suite. He trembled and raised quivering hands in supplication. "Please, please, don't hurt me. I had—had nothing to do with all this. They forced me to sign things, to order up the militia. I—I'm innocent," the governor blubbered.

"And pigs build nests in trees," Holten responded in a bored tone. Three troopers entered, and Eli gestured to the governor. "Get this pile of dung out of here."

Two of the cavalrymen took the governor by the shoulders and lifted him. They started for the door. Sudden energy charged the corrupt politician, and he broke away from them. Swiftly he turned on Eli Holten.

"It's all your fault!" he screamed. "I told them you and Corrington had to be killed first. I'll not go to prison. Not for this!" he raved as he triggered the tiny derringer in his right hand.

The under-powered .41 rimfire made a flat pop. Its slug struck Eli Holten's thick, leather belt, penetrating through it and his trousers and broke the skin of his lower abdomen. Impact and pain doubled the scout over so that his Remington discharged at a downward angle. The slub smacked into the governor's pampered, well-fed body and burst his bladder. It veered then and ricocheted around his pelvic girdle, to exit out the front, taking his manhood with it.

By then the troopers had grabbed him again, and Governor Stratton hung slackly in their grasp. He died of internal hemorrhaging while he wailed in horror over his emasculation.

Choking back the rising bile, Eli Holten left the suite and walked hurriedly out of the bordello. In the clear, fresh air and warm, welcoming sunshine of the main street, he sucked in huge breaths and wondered at the madness induced by greed. Everyone had lost in this one, and he knew that the images of horror from inside the whorehouse would haunt him for as long as he lived.

"Eli, I want you to come back to Dakota," Frank Corrington pressed earnestly.

Seated in a chair in his convalescent room, the general patted the blanket that covered his pajama-clad legs. "I'll be up and around in another week according to that pill-rolling fraud, Jansen. We'll take off somewhere, go fishing, drink ourselves blind, chase girls."

"I'll do that gladly. But I still feel that I should return to Arizona. The Apaches fascinate me. They're . . . unlike any other Indians. And General Crook has his hands full. He needs me."

"*I* need you, Eli," Corrington blurted, a catch in his voice.

"Frank—Frank, there's just too damned much 'civilization' around here. Telegraph, telephone, next thing you know, we'll have the Women's Temperance Union out here banging their stupid drums and drying up all the saloons. I must be getting older. In fact, I know I am. You mentioned chasing girls, and the reason I'm here so early is because I'm hiding out. There are certain, ah, girls chasing me."

His words might have been a cue. A sudden banging

222

came at the door, which flew open before the general could respond, and admitted Melissa and Samantha Thorne. They flew to Eli in a flutter of skirts.

"Oh, *there* you are. You come along with us right this minute. Why, we hardly got, ah, anything done this morning," Melissa complained.

"You down-right disappoint us, Eli," Samantha added.

With General Corrington laughing in the background, Melissa and Samantha gabbled and cackled as they drug Eli away.

A week went by in the steamy bed of Eli's cabin. He awakened in the middle of the night to fluttery lips—five pair of them!—nuzzling his body hungrily, and soft, inquisitive fingers—fifty of them!—exploring his face, his chest, his belly, legs and groin. His well-used—Eli would say *over*-used—phallus responded yet another time, pulsing as it filled and elongated.

One half of a pair of twins reared up out of the covers and straddled him. Slowly she inched down on his throbbing organ, tightly encasing it in hot, moist membranes. She shivered, and her taut, young breasts bobbed and swayed. Was it Sam? Was it Susie? For the time being, Holten didn't care. With little squeals of delight she filled her passage with all of him. Another figure, smaller than the others, squirmed and wormed its way atop his chest. He smelled the heady muck of aroused womanhood, kissed the soft mound, and touched the sensitive fronds within with his tongue.

Sighing happily, little Helen flattened her tiny breasts against Eli's belly and began to lap at the exposed length of his phallus as it slid back and forth in the happy twin's sublime container. Three other delightful feminine voices raised in impatient protest.

"When do we get our turn?"

223

Maybe, Eli thought, in a pink foam of ecstasy, maybe he had been foredoomed to be loved to death by five lovely young women at the same time. With lips and tongues and wet little chubs, the five Thorne delights spent the night doing their damnedest to prove him right.